PENGUIN CLASSICS
Maigret's Madwoman

'I love reading Simenon. He makes me think of Chekhov'
– William Faulkner

'A truly wonderful writer, marvellously readable – lucid, simple, absolutely in tune with the world he creates'
– Muriel Spark

'Few writers have ever conveyed with such a sure touch, the bleakness of human life'
– A. N. Wilson

'One of the greatest writers of the twentieth century. Simenon was unequalled at making us look inside, though the ability was masked by his brilliance at absorbing us obsessively in his stories'
– *Guardian*

'A novelist who entered his fictional world as if he were part of it'
– Peter Ackroyd

'The greatest of all, the most genuine novelist we have had in literature'
– André Gide

'Superb. The most addictive of writers. A unique teller of tales'
– *Observer*

'The mysteries of the human personality are revealed in all their disconcerting complexity'
– Anita Brookner

'A writer who, more than any other crime novelist, combined a high literary reputation with popular appeal'
– P. D. James

'A supreme writer. Unforgettable vividness'
– *Independent*

'Compelling, remorseless, brilliant'
– John Gray

'Extraordinary masterpieces of the twentieth century'
– John Banville

Georges Simenon was born on 12 February 1903 in Liège, Belgium, and died in 1989 in Lausanne, Switzerland, where he had lived for the latter part of his life. Between 1931 and 1972 he published seventy-five novels and twenty-eight short stories featuring Inspector Maigret.

Simenon always resisted identifying himself with his famous literary character, but acknowledged that they shared an important characteristic:

> My motto, to the extent that I have one, has been noted often enough, and I've always conformed to it. It's the one I've given to old Maigret, who resembles me in certain points: 'understand and judge not'.

Penguin is publishing the entire series of Maigret novels.

GEORGES SIMENON

Maigret's Madwoman

Translated by SIÂN REYNOLDS

PENGUIN BOOKS

PENGUIN CLASSICS

UK | USA | Canada | Ireland | Australia
India | New Zealand | South Africa

Penguin Books is part of the Penguin Random House group of companies
whose addresses can be found at global.penguinrandomhouse.com.

First published in serial, as *La folle de Maigret*, in *Le Figaro* 1970
First published in book form by Presses de la Cité 1970
This translation first published 2019
002

Set in 12.5/15 pt Dante MT Std
Typeset by Jouve (UK), Milton Keynes
Printed and bound in Great Britain by Clays Ltd, Elcograf S.p.A.

ISBN: 978-0-241-30430-3

www.greenpenguin.co.uk

MIX
Paper from
responsible sources
FSC® C018179

Penguin Random House is committed to a
sustainable future for our business, our readers
and our planet. This book is made from Forest
Stewardship Council® certified paper.

Maigret's Madwoman

1.

Duty Officer Picot was standing to the left of the arched doorway at Quai des Orfèvres, with his colleague Latuile to the right. It was about ten o'clock. On this May morning, the sun was shining and Paris was bathed in pastel colours.

At some point, Picot noticed her, but without paying much attention: a frail little old lady, wearing a white hat, white cotton gloves and a grey dress. Her legs, slightly bowed with age, were very thin.

Was she carrying a shopping bag or a handbag? He couldn't remember. He hadn't seen her arrive. She had stopped on the pavement a few steps away from him and was peering into the courtyard of the Police Judiciaire, where the small staff cars were parked.

There are often curious onlookers, especially tourists, who come to peep inside police headquarters like that. She ventured as far as the entrance, looked the officer up and down, then turned round and walked away towards the Pont-Neuf.

Next day, Picot was once more on duty, and at about the same time of day he saw her again. On this occasion, after hesitating for quite a while, she walked up to him and spoke:

'This is where Inspector Maigret has his office, isn't it?'

'Yes, madame. On the first floor.'

She looked up at the windows. She had very delicate and fine-drawn features, and her light grey eyes seemed to have a constant expression of surprise.

'Thank you, officer.'

She turned away, and it was a shopping bag she was carrying, which led him to think she must live nearby.

The following day, Picot was off duty. The officer replacing him paid no attention to the little old woman who slipped inside the courtyard. She cast about for a moment before taking the door on the left and starting up the stairs. On the first floor, the long corridor intimidated her, and she seemed rather lost. Old Joseph, the usher, went up to her and asked in a kindly voice:

'Were you looking for something?'

'Inspector Maigret's office.'

'You want to speak to Inspector Maigret?'

'Yes. That's why I'm here.'

'Have you been sent a summons?'

She shook her head, looking distressed.

'Do you have to have a summons?'

'Would you like to leave him a message?'

'I need to speak to him personally. It's very important.'

'If you fill in this form for me, I'll see if the inspector is able to receive you.'

She sat down at the table with its green baize cloth. There was a strong smell of fresh paint in the offices, which had recently been redecorated. She did not know this and thought that for an official institution the atmosphere was quite cheerful.

She tore up the first form. She wrote slowly, pausing over every word and underlining some of them. The second form went into the waste paper basket too, and then a third, and only at the fourth attempt did she seem satisfied, before going across to Joseph.

'You will deliver this into his own hands, won't you?'

'Yes, madame.'

'I suppose he's very busy?'

'Yes, very.'

'Do you think he will see me?'

'That I don't know, madame.'

She was over eighty, possibly eighty-six or seven, and she could have weighed hardly more than a child. Her body seemed refined by the passage of time, and her skin was almost translucent. She was smiling timidly, as if to try to flirt with old Joseph.

'Please do what you can. It's so very important to me!'

'Take a seat here, madame.'

He went towards one of the doors, on which he tapped. Maigret was conferring with Lapointe and Janvier, both of whom were on their feet; sounds from the outside world were reaching them through the wide open window.

Maigret accepted the form, glanced at it and frowned.

'What's she like?'

'A very proper old lady, a bit shy. She asked me to insist that you see her.'

On the top line, she had written her name in quite firm and regular handwriting: *Mme Antoine de Caramé*.

The address she had given was 8a, Quai de la Mégisserie.

As the reason for her visit, she had put:

Wishes to tell Inspector Maigret something of the utmost importance. It is a matter of life and death.

By this point, the handwriting had become more shaky and the lines less straight. Some words were underlined: 'Inspector', then 'utmost importance'. And 'a matter of life and death' was underlined twice.

'Is this some madwoman?' Maigret muttered, puffing at his pipe.

'She doesn't look like it. She seemed very composed.'

At Quai des Orfèvres, they were used to receiving letters from people who were mad, or at least half mad. And almost always, they contained some words heavily underlined.

'Could you see her, Lapointe? If you don't, she'll be turning up here every morning.'

A few moments later, the old lady was being shown into the small office at the end of the corridor. Lapointe was there alone, standing by the window.

'Come in, madame, and please take a seat.'

Looking at him curiously, she asked:

'Are you his son?'

'Whose son?'

'Inspector Maigret's.'

'No, madame. I'm Inspector Lapointe.'

'But you're just a boy!'

'I'm twenty-seven.'

This was true, but it was also true that he appeared to be no more than twenty-two and was often mistaken for a student rather than a police officer.

'But it was Inspector Maigret I wanted to see.'

'Unfortunately, he's too busy just now to receive you.'

She hesitated, fiddled with her white handbag and seemed unable to make up her mind to sit down.

'Perhaps if I came back tomorrow?'

'It would be the same thing.'

'Does Inspector Maigret never see anyone?'

'Only in very important cases.'

'But this *is* a very important case. It's a matter of life and death.'

'That's what you wrote on the form.'

'Yes, I did, so . . .'

'If you could just tell me what it's about, I'll pass it on to Inspector Maigret myself, and he can decide.'

'And then, perhaps he'll see me?'

'I can't make any promises, but it's not impossible.'

She seemed to be weighing up the pros and cons for a long while and finally decided to perch on the edge of a chair, facing Lapointe who had sat down behind the desk.

'So what's this about?'

'First of all, I should tell you that I have lived in the same apartment for forty-two years, on Quai de la Mégisserie. On the ground floor, there's a shop that sells birds, and when their cages are out on the pavement they sing all day. So they keep me company.'

'But you were referring to some danger.'

'I certainly am in some danger, but you'll assume I'm making things up. Young people tend to think that old people aren't right in the head any more.'

'The thought hadn't occurred to me.'

'I don't know how to explain it to you. Since the death of my second husband, twelve years ago, I have lived alone and no one ever comes into my apartment. It's too big for me now, all on my own, but I intend to stay there until I die. I'm eighty-six, and I don't need anyone to help me cook and clean.'

'Do you have any pets? A dog or a cat?'

'No. As I told you, I hear all the birds singing downstairs, because I'm on the first floor.'

'So what is troubling you, madame?'

'It's hard to say. But five times at least, in the last couple of weeks, some of my things have been moved about.'

'What do you mean? When you come home, you find they're not in the same place as when you went out?'

'That's right. Perhaps a picture frame is crooked, or a vase is the wrong way round.'

'Are you quite sure that you are remembering correctly?'

'You see! Because I'm old, you're already doubting my memory. But as I told you, I've lived in the same apartment for forty-two years. So I know exactly where all my things are.'

'But nothing has been stolen? Nothing has disappeared?'

'No, inspector.'

'Do you keep any money in the house?'

'Very little. Just enough for my needs every month. My first husband worked at the City Council offices, and he left me a pension I can draw on regularly. I have some money put by in the Savings Bank as well.'

'Do you own any valuable objects – pictures, ornaments, anything like that?'

'I've got some things I'm attached to, but they don't necessarily have any market value.'

'And your visitor, man or woman, hasn't left any telltale signs? For instance, if it was raining, you might have seen footprints.'

'But it hasn't rained for over ten days.'

'Or cigarette ash, perhaps?'

'No.'

'Does anyone else have a key to your apartment?'

'No, I keep my key in my handbag and it's the only one.'

He looked at her with some embarrassment.

'So in short, you've come to complain simply that some objects in your home are slightly out of place.'

'That's right.'

'And you've never surprised anyone there?'

'No, never.'

'And you've no idea who it could be?'

'No.'

'Do you have children?'

'No, unfortunately, I never had any.'

'Other relations?'

'I have a niece who is a professional masseuse, but I don't see her very often, although she lives just the other side of the Seine.'

'What about friends? Men, women?'

'Most of the people I used to know have died. And that isn't all.'

She was speaking normally, without emphasis, and her gaze was steady.

'I'm being followed.'

'You mean someone is following you in the street?'

'Yes.'

'Have you seen whoever is following you?'

'I've seen various people, when I have turned round suddenly, but I don't know which one it can be.'

'Do you often leave the house?'

'Yes, in the morning, first thing. At about eight o'clock, I go shopping in the neighbourhood. I'm sorry the central market isn't there any more in Les Halles, because it was so close and I was used to it. Since they knocked it down, I've tried different shops, but it's not the same.'

'Is the person who follows you a man?'

'That I don't know.'

'I suppose you're back by about ten o'clock?'

'Yes, I sit by the window and peel my vegetables.'

'Do you stay at home in the afternoon?'

'Only when it's raining or too cold. Otherwise, I go and sit on a bench, almost always in the Tuileries Gardens. I'm not the only person who's adopted a bench. There are other people, about my age, that I've been seeing for years in the same place.'

'Are you being followed all the way to the Tuileries?'

'Someone follows me when I go out. It's as if they want to be sure I won't be coming home again straight away.'

'And have you sometimes?'

'Three times. I pretended I'd forgotten something, and went back up to my apartment.'

'And there was nobody there, of course.'

'All the same, other times, objects have been moved. Somebody doesn't like me, I've no idea why. I've never done any harm to anyone. Perhaps there are several of them.'

'What was your husband's job at the Council offices?'

'My first husband was a chief clerk. He had a lot of responsibility. Unfortunately, he died young, of a heart attack, at forty-five.'

'And you married again?'

'Over ten years later. My second husband was in charge of a department at the Bazar de l'Hôtel de Ville, selling gardening implements and tools.'

'And he also died?'

'He'd been retired a long time by then. If he was still alive today, he'd be ninety-two.'

'And when did he die?'

'I thought I'd already told you that: twelve years ago.'

'And he didn't have any family? Was he a widower when you married him?'

'He just had one son, who lives in Venezuela.'

'Look, madame, I'm going to tell Inspector Maigret what you have just told me.'

'And you think he'll see me?'

'If he does decide to see you, he'll send you an appointment.'

'You have my address?'

'Yes, it's on the form, isn't it?'

'Yes, that's true, I was forgetting. You see, I have such trust in him. I'm convinced he's the only person who will understand me. I'm not saying this to be rude to you, but you do look a little young.'

He escorted her to the door and then along the corridor to the big staircase.

When he went back to Maigret's office, Janvier was no longer there.

'Well?'

'I think you were right, chief. Yes, she is mad. But it's a quiet kind of madness, she's very calm, very in control. She's eighty-six, and I'd like to be in that kind of shape when I'm her age.'

'So what's this great danger she's in?'

'She's lived for forty years or more in the same apartment on Quai de la Mégisserie. She was married twice and widowed twice. She claims that when she goes out, her objects get moved around.'

Maigret relit his pipe.

'What kind of objects?'

'Well, she might find a picture frame crooked, or some ornament that isn't facing the same way as before.'

'She doesn't have a dog or a cat?'

'No, she's content to hear the birds singing in the shop downstairs.'

'Nothing else?'

'Yes. She's convinced she's being followed.'

'Has she spotted anyone?'

'No, that's the thing, but she's absolutely sure about it.'

'Is she likely to come here again?'

'She's determined to see you personally. In her eyes, you're God Almighty, and apparently you're the only person who will understand her. What should I do?'

'Nothing.'

'She'll be back.'

'Well, we'll see then. But you could just go and ask the concierge at that address a few questions.'

And Maigret picked up once more the file he had been

studying, while young Lapointe returned to the inspectors' office.

'Was she a madwoman?' Janvier asked him.

'Probably, but not like the usual ones.'

'Do you know many mad people?'

'One of my aunts is in a psychiatric hospital.'

'I'm guessing this old woman made something of an impression on you.'

'Yes, maybe she did, a little. She kept looking at me as if I was just a kid and unable to understand. The only person she trusts is Maigret.'

After lunch, Lapointe went over to Quai de la Mégisserie, where most of the shops sold caged birds and small animals. On this sunny afternoon, the cafés had put tables out on the terraces. Looking up, Lapointe saw that the windows on the first floor were open. He had some difficulty finding the concierge's lodge, which was at the far end of the courtyard. The concierge, sitting in a patch of sunlight, was darning a pair of men's socks.

He showed her his police badge.

'Who did you want?'

'Can you tell me what you know about Madame Antoine de Caramé? Is that the right name? An old lady who lives on the first floor.'

'Yes, I know who you mean. Antoine was really the surname of her *second* husband, so officially she's plain Madame Antoine. But since she's very proud of her first husband, who was something important in the Council offices, she calls herself Madame Antoine de Caramé.'

'What's she like?'

'What do you mean?'

'Well, is she a little odd?'

'I certainly wonder why the police are interested in her all of a sudden.'

'Actually, she came to us.'

'What did she have to complain about?'

'Apparently when she goes out, things in her apartment are moved around. She hasn't mentioned it to you?'

'No, she just asked me if I had seen any strangers go up there. I told her I hadn't. But in any case, I can't see people coming and going: the staircase is at the end of the corridor.'

'Does anyone visit her?'

'Her niece comes round once or twice a month. But sometimes it can be three months without her calling.'

'So, would you say the old lady behaves just like anyone else?'

'Well, like all old women who live alone. In her case, she's obviously received a good education and she's polite to everyone.'

'Is she there at the moment?'

'No. The slightest bit of sun and she's off. She's probably sitting on a bench in the Tuileries Gardens.'

'Does she ever chat with you?'

'Just a few words in passing. She mostly asks after my husband, who's in hospital.'

'Thank you for your time.'

'I suppose I'd better not tell her you were here?'

'It doesn't matter.'

'At any rate, I wouldn't say she's mad. She has her funny

little ways, like all old people, but no more than anyone else.'

'I may be back to see you again.'

Maigret was in a cheerful mood. Not a drop of rain had fallen in ten days, there was a light breeze, a blue sky and in this ideal month of May, Paris was as colourful as the set of a musical comedy.

He stayed a little longer in his office, checking a report that had lain there a while and which he wanted to be finished with. He could hear cars and buses going past, and every now and then the hooter of a tug-boat.

It was almost seven o'clock when he opened the door of the neighbouring office, where Lucas was on duty with two or three other inspectors, and wished them goodnight.

On the way downstairs, he wondered whether he might call in at the Brasserie Dauphine for an aperitif and had still not made up his mind as he went through the doorway past the two officers on duty, who saluted him.

In the end, he decided he would rather go straight home and had only taken a few steps towards Boulevard du Palais when a diminutive figure appeared in front of him. He immediately recognized her from the description Lapointe had given him.

'It is you, isn't it?' she asked eagerly.

She didn't even say his name. It could only be him, the famous Detective Chief Inspector Maigret, all of whose cases she had followed in the newspapers. She had even cut out articles about him, which she pasted into scrapbooks.

'I must beg your pardon for coming up to you in the street like this, but upstairs they wouldn't let me through.'

Maigret felt a little ridiculous and could well imagine the ironic looks of the two policemen behind him.

'I understand, of course. I don't blame them. You have to be left in peace to work, don't you?'

What struck Maigret most forcefully was the colour of her eyes, pale grey, a sort of washed-out grey, both gentle and sparkling at the same time. She was smiling at him. Clearly she was in seventh heaven. But at the same time, an extraordinary energy could be sensed in that frail body.

'Which way are you going?'

He pointed towards the Pont Saint-Michel.

'Would you mind if I walked with you as far as that?'

Trotting alongside him, she looked even tinier.

'The important thing, you see, is that you must understand I'm not mad. I know what young people think about the old, and I am a very old woman.'

'You're eighty-six, is that right?'

'I see that the young man who interviewed me has told you about me. He seems very young for the job he's in, but he's well brought up and very courteous.'

'Have you been waiting outside long?'

'Since five to six. I thought you would be leaving your office at six o'clock. I saw a lot of gentlemen come out, but you weren't among them.'

So she had been waiting a whole hour, on her feet, under the indifferent gaze of the policemen outside the doorway.

'I feel as if I'm in danger. There must be a reason why

someone is coming into my apartment and searching my things.'

'How do you know that someone is searching your things?'

'Because I don't find them back in their exact place. I'm obsessive about tidiness. In my home, every object has had its precise place for over forty years.'

'And this has happened several times?'

'At least four times.'

'Do you own any valuables?'

'No, inspector. Just the little things you acquire over your lifetime and keep for sentimental reasons.'

She turned round quickly, and he asked:

'Is someone following you now?'

'No, not now. I beg you, please come and see me. You'll understand better when you're on the spot.'

'I'll do my very best to find a free moment.'

'Do more than that. Quai de la Mégisserie is only a little way from here. In the next few days, come and see me, and I promise I won't keep you. And I promise I won't turn up at your office again.'

In fact, she was quite artful.

'I'll be along some time soon.'

'This week?'

'Perhaps this week. Or if not, at the beginning of next.'

He had arrived at his bus stop.

'Now you must excuse me, but I should be getting home.'

'I'm counting on you,' she said. 'I trust you.'

He would have found it difficult at that moment to

say what he thought of her. Certainly, her story was exactly the kind that is invented by fantasists, with complete sincerity. But standing in front of her, looking her in the face, he was tempted to take her tale seriously.

He went home, where the table was laid for dinner, and kissed his wife on both cheeks.

'I hope you managed to get outside in this beautiful weather.'

'I ran a few errands.'

Then he asked her a question that surprised her:

'Do you ever find yourself sitting on a bench in the park?'

She had to think back.

'I must do sometimes, waiting for a dentist's appointment, for instance.'

'This evening I had a visitor, a lady who spends almost every afternoon sitting on a bench in the Tuileries.'

'There are plenty of people like that.'

'Does anyone ever speak to you?'

'I can think of one time. A mother with a little girl, who asked me to look after the child for a few minutes while she went to buy something on the other side of the gardens.'

The window was open here too. For dinner, as on the finest summer days, they ate cold meats, salad and mayonnaise.

'Shall we go for a little walk?'

The sunset was still painting the sky pink and Boulevard Richard-Lenoir was quiet; here and there, people were leaning on their window-sills to take the air.

They walked simply for walking's sake, for the pleasure of being together, but without having anything particular to say. They looked at the same passers-by, the same shop windows, and from time to time one of them would make a remark. They went round by Bastille and returned along Boulevard Beaumarchais.

'I had a strange old lady come to see me today. Or rather she saw Lapointe. But she waited for me outside on the embankment, and caught me as I went past. If you listen to her story, she sounds mad. Or a bit deranged anyway.'

'Why, what's happened to her?'

'Nothing. Only she claims that when she gets back home after going out, some of her things have been moved from their proper place.'

'Does she have a cat?'

'That's what Lapointe asked her. No, no pets. She lives just above one of the shops where they sell caged birds and that's enough for her, because she hears them singing all day.'

'And do you think she's telling the truth?'

'As long she was in front of me, yes, I thought so. She has light grey eyes and they seem to shine with sincerity and goodness. I might even say a certain simplicity of soul. She's been widowed for twelve years, lives alone. Apart from a niece she sees only rarely, there's no other family.

'Every morning, she does her shopping in the neighbourhood, wearing her white hat and white gloves. And in the afternoon, she usually goes to sit on a bench in the Tuileries. She doesn't complain about her life. She's not bored. Doesn't seem to feel lonely.'

'There are plenty of old people like that, you know.'

'I'm sure there are, but there's something different about her that I can't put my finger on.'

By the time they got home, night had fallen and the air was cooler. They went to bed early and next morning, since the weather was still fine, Maigret decided to walk to the office.

A pile of correspondence awaited him as usual. He had time to go through it and have a word with his inspectors before attending the daily briefing. There was nothing important in hand.

He spent quite an ordinary morning, decided to have lunch on Place Dauphine and telephoned his wife to say he would not be back at midday. After his meal, he was on the point of crossing the Pont-Neuf to go to Quai de la Mégisserie. A chance incident prevented him. He met on the pavement a former colleague, now retired, and they chatted for about a quarter of an hour, standing in the sunshine.

Twice more during the afternoon, he thought about the old lady, whom his inspectors had already christened 'Maigret's old madwoman'. Both times, he postponed his visit, thinking he would go there later, the next day, for instance.

The newspapers would surely make fun of him if they ever got hold of this story about objects changing places.

That evening, they watched television. The following morning, he went to the office by bus, since he was late. It was almost midday when he received a call from the chief of police in the first arrondissement.

'I've got a case here which must be of interest to your

squad, because the concierge tells me one of your inspectors, a handsome young man apparently, was round asking questions a couple of days ago.'

He had a sudden sense of foreboding.

'Quai de la Mégisserie?'

'Yes.'

'She's dead?'

'Yes.'

'Are you at the scene now?'

'I'm on the ground floor with the bird-seller, because there's no phone in the apartment.'

'I'm on my way.'

Lapointe was in the next office.

'Come with me.'

'Something serious, chief?'

'For you and me, yes. The old lady.'

'The one with the white hat and the grey eyes?'

'Yes. She's dead.'

'Murdered?'

'I suppose so, otherwise the local police chief wouldn't have called me.'

They didn't take a car, since it was quicker to walk. Chief Inspector Jenton, whom Maigret knew well, was waiting for them on the pavement, standing next to a cockatoo attached to its perch by a chain.

'You know her?'

'I met her only the once. I'd promised to call on her one of these days. I almost came yesterday.'

Would it have changed anything?

'Is there someone upstairs?'

'One of my men and Doctor Forniaux, who's just arrived.'

'How did she die?'

'I don't know yet. A neighbour from the second floor noticed that her door was ajar at about half past ten. She didn't think anything of it and went out shopping. When she returned at eleven, the door was still open, so she called out: "Madame Antoine! Madame Antoine! Are you there? . . ."'

'And since there was no reply, she pushed the door further open and almost tripped over the body.'

'On the floor?'

'Yes, just inside the sitting room. So the neighbour rang the police at once.'

Maigret climbed the stairs slowly, and his expression was serious.

'What's she wearing?'

'She's still got the white hat and gloves she'd put on to go out.'

'No apparent wound?'

'Not that I saw. The concierge said one of your men was here a day or two ago, asking about her, so I contacted you immediately.'

Doctor Forniaux, on his knees beside the body, stood up as the three men entered the room.

They shook hands.

'You've identified the cause of death?'

'Suffocation.'

'You mean she was strangled?'

'No. They must have used some cloth, a towel or a

handkerchief even, and clamped it over her nose and mouth until she died.'

'You're sure about that?'

'I'll confirm it after the post-mortem.'

The window was wide open, and they could hear the chirruping of the birds down below.

'And when do you estimate it happened?'

'Yesterday, either late afternoon or evening.'

The old lady looked even frailer dead than alive. Just a small body, with one leg oddly bent, which gave her the appearance of a disjointed puppet.

The doctor had closed her eyes. Her face and hands were as white as ivory.

'How long do you think it would have taken to kill her like that?'

'Hard to be precise. Especially given her age. Five minutes? A bit more or a bit less.'

'Lapointe, phone the prosecutor's office and the lab. Tell Moers to send a team over.'

'You don't need me any more, do you?' asked the doctor. 'I'll send the van round so that she can be taken to the Forensic Institute as soon as you've finished here.'

The local police chief sent his man downstairs, where a small group of people had gathered.

'Tell them to move on. This isn't a circus.'

They were both long accustomed to crime scenes. But they were nonetheless taken aback by this one, perhaps because it was a very old lady, and perhaps too because there was no evident injury.

And then there was the setting, which dated from the

early years of the twentieth century or even from the nineteenth. The heavy furniture was made of mahogany, massive and lovingly polished, the armchairs upholstered in crimson velvet, the kind you can still see in some provincial front parlours. There were numerous ornaments, and framed photographs on the walls, which were papered in a flowered design.

'We have to wait for the prosecutor's office to send someone.'

'They'll be along soon. We'll get one of the duty deputies with a clerk. He'll just take a look round and that'll be that.'

This was indeed the way things happened as a rule. Afterwards, the experts would move in with their cumbersome apparatus.

The door behind them opened quietly and Maigret gave a start. It was a little girl, who presumably lived on one of the other floors and had heard a noise.

'Do you often come in here?'

'No. I've never been in before.'

'Where do you live?'

'Across the landing.'

'Did you know Madame Antoine?'

'I sometimes saw her on the stairs.'

'Did she talk to you?'

'She used to smile at me.'

'She didn't give you sweets or chocolate?'

'No.'

'Where's your mother?'

'In the kitchen.'

'Will you take me to see her?'

He made his excuses to the local inspector.

'Please let me know when the prosecutor arrives.'

It was an old building. The walls and ceilings had long been out of true, and there were gaps in the parquet floors.

'Mama, a gentleman wants to talk to you.'

The woman came out of the kitchen wiping her hands on her apron. There were some soap suds still at her elbow.

'I'm Inspector Maigret. By chance, I saw your daughter push open the door across the way. Was it you who found the body?'

'What body? Lucette, go to your room.'

'Your neighbour's.'

'She's dead? I always said that would happen one day. At her age, people shouldn't be living alone. She must have felt unwell and couldn't call anyone.'

'No, she was murdered.'

'I didn't hear a thing. Of course there's a lot of noise out on the street.'

'It wasn't a gunshot, and it didn't happen this morning but yesterday afternoon or evening.'

'Ah, poor woman! She was a bit stuck-up for my taste, but I had nothing against her.'

'Were you on good terms?'

'I don't think we've exchanged ten sentences in the seven years we've been living here.'

'You don't know anything about her life?'

'I'd sometimes see her going out in the morning. In winter she wore a black hat, in summer a white one, and she always had gloves on, even to go shopping. But that was her own business, I suppose.'

'Did she have visitors?'

'Not to my knowledge. Oh, wait, I've two or three times seen a woman ring the bell, rather a stocky woman, mannish-looking.'

'During the day?'

'No, in the evening. Just after supper.'

'And recently, you haven't noticed any unusual comings and goings in the building?'

'There are always people coming and going, it's like a railway station. The concierge just stays in her lodge across the yard and doesn't bother with the tenants.'

She turned towards her daughter, who had sidled in again silently.

'What did I tell you? Back to your room, miss.'

'I'll be seeing you again, because I need to interview all the tenants.'

'I suppose you don't know who did it?'

'No.'

'How did they find her?'

'Someone from the second floor saw the door open. And as it was still open an hour later, she called out Madame Antoine's name and went in.'

'I can guess who *that* was.'

'Why?'

'Because she's the nosiest person in the building. You'll see, it'll have been that Rochin woman.'

They heard steps on the stairs and Maigret went to meet the prosecutor's men, who were just arriving.

'This way,' he said. 'Doctor Forniaux was here, but he's busy this morning, so he had to leave.'

The deputy was a tall young man, suave and elegantly dressed. He looked around in surprise, as if he had never before seen an interior of this kind. Then he glanced briefly at the huddled grey form on the carpet.

'Do we know how she was killed?'

'Suffocation.'

'Well, obviously she wouldn't have been able to put up much of a fight.'

Examining Magistrate Libart arrived in turn, and he too looked around the room with curiosity.

'It's like being in an old film,' he remarked.

Lapointe had come back upstairs and his eyes encountered Maigret's. They did not shrug their shoulders, but thought the same thing nevertheless.

2.

'Perhaps I'd better send you two or three uniformed officers to keep onlookers away,' suggested the local inspector.

The tenants were already assembling on the stairs and landing. The men from the prosecutor's office did not stay long, and the forensic team took the body away on a covered stretcher.

Lapointe had not failed to notice how pale Maigret was and how serious his expression. Three days earlier, Maigret had not known the woman who had died, he'd never even heard of her. But in her distress, whether imagined or real, it was to him that she had turned. She had tried to reach him personally because she trusted him, and he could still see her approaching him on the pavement, her eyes shining in admiration.

He had assumed she was mad, or at least somewhat deranged. But a vague unease had nevertheless persisted in his mind, deep down, and he had promised her he would call round. And he would have come, perhaps this very afternoon.

It was too late now. She had been murdered, no doubt about it, exactly as she had feared.

'Get fingerprints from all the rooms, on all the objects, even those that are very unlikely to have been touched.'

He heard a burst of noise on the landing and opened

the front door. A dozen or so reporters and photographers were outside, with a uniformed policeman preventing them from entering the apartment.

Someone thrust a microphone in his face.

'What sort of crime is this, inspector?'

'As of now, we don't know anything about it, gentlemen. You might say the investigation has not yet begun.'

'Who was it?'

'An old lady.'

'Madame Antoine de Caramé, the concierge told us. And she says someone was round here at the beginning of the week from the Police Judiciaire, asking questions about her. Why was that? Did you have reason to believe she was at risk?'

'All I can tell you at the moment is that we don't know anything.'

'She lived alone, didn't she? And never had any visitors?'

'As far as we know, that is correct. But there's a niece, whose name I don't yet have, who sometimes came to see her. She is a masseuse by profession and lives not far from here, across the Seine.'

The radio station had recorded this brief statement. And it would appear in the evening papers. So the niece would probably make herself known to them once she heard the news.

'Can we take any pictures inside?'

'No, not yet, the Criminal Records people are still working there. And now, I must ask you to clear the stairway, please.'

'We'll be waiting in the courtyard.'

Maigret shut the door and finally walked round the apartment. The room facing out to the front was the sitting room, where Madame Antoine had been attacked, no doubt when she came back from her usual outing to the Tuileries.

Had someone been visiting the apartment in her absence, as she had suspected? Probably. But what could they have been looking for? What could this place conceal that would explain such determination?

Presumably she had returned home sooner than expected, and the intruder, being surprised, had decided to get rid of her.

Surely that meant that she knew the attacker? Otherwise, wouldn't the visitor simply have run off? Did he need to kill her?

'Fingerprints?'

'So far, only the old lady's. And on the table in the sitting room, the doctor's, we're starting to recognize those.'

There were two windows in the sitting room, which was low-ceilinged like the rest of the first floor. A door led to the dining room, as old-fashioned as the rest, and as was the old lady herself. In a corner, on a marble-topped table, was an enormous houseplant in an earthenware pot wrapped in fabric.

Everywhere there was the same tidiness, the same meticulous cleanliness.

The dining room had only one window, and opposite this was a door leading to the kitchen. The bread bin contained a baguette, still fresh. In the refrigerator, Maigret found several small packets, one containing a slice of ham, another half a cutlet. There was also a lettuce and half a bottle of milk.

Only one room remained, the bedroom, and like the kitchen it looked on to the courtyard. Here there was an immense mirrored wardrobe made of walnut: the bed and other pieces of furniture were in the same wood. On the floor was a vaguely oriental carpet, its colours faded, and threadbare in patches.

The whole place breathed a certain air of dignity. Later, this afternoon perhaps, he would have to come back to check all the objects one by one, including the contents of cupboards and drawers.

'We've finished now, chief.'

The photographers were taking away their equipment. As for the fingerprints, they had still found none, other than those of the old lady.

Maigret gave instructions to the uniformed policeman not to let anyone in except the inspector he would be sending. He went down the dark stairwell with its worn steps and its bannister polished by two or three centuries of use.

In the courtyard, journalists and photographers were besieging the concierge, who was answering them ill-humouredly. Lapointe was following Maigret without speaking. He too was shocked. He could still visualize Madame Antoine in the little office where he had interviewed her, and where he had decided that she was perhaps wandering in her wits.

The bird-seller, Monsieur Caille, if they were to believe the name on the shopfront, was standing alongside his cages, wearing a grey canvas overall.

'May I use your phone?'

'Yes, of course, Monsieur Maigret.'

He was smiling knowingly, proud of having recognized the inspector. The telephone was inside the shop, where there were other birdcages piled one on top of another, as well as goldfish in several tanks. An elderly man, also in grey overalls, was feeding them.

'Hello . . . Lucas? . . . I need someone down here, Quai de la Mégisserie, 8a . . . Janvier? . . . yes, that's fine . . . He's to come inside the flat and not let anyone else in . . . And can you phone my wife to tell her I won't be home for lunch?'

When he hung up, he turned towards the old bird-seller.

'Have you lived in this building a long time?'

'Since my own father brought us here when I was only ten.'

'So you would have known Madame Antoine when she moved in?'

'It must be about forty years ago. Her first husband, Monsieur de Caramé, was still alive. A good-looking man, rather impressive. He had some important job at the City Council offices and when there was a big do on there, he always gave us tickets.'

'In those days, did they see many people?'

'There were two or three couples, friends of theirs, who came round nearly every week to play cards.'

'And what was Madame Antoine like then?'

'Sweet, pretty. But there you are, fate plays funny tricks. To look at her, you'd think her health was fair to middling, and that she wouldn't make old bones, she was such a thin little thing. Whereas he was the opposite, big chap, well-covered, never known him have a day's illness. Liked his food. But he was the one who died suddenly, in his office. And until yesterday, his wife was still alive.'

'And she married again soon afterwards?'

'No, no, she was on her own for about ten years. Then she met Monsieur Antoine, I don't know where, and she ended up marrying him. I've got nothing against him. Perfectly all right, but not as distinguished as the first husband.

'He worked in the Bazar de l'Hôtel de Ville, and I think he was in charge of a whole department. He was a widower. And he had a little workshop upstairs where he made things. That was his hobby, he loved it. Didn't say much. Just good morning, good evening. And they didn't go out a lot either.

'He had a car and, on Sundays, he took his wife out to the country. In summer, they went somewhere near Étretat.'

'Would there be any other tenants who knew them?'

'I'm afraid I'm probably the last one. The others have all died one after another, and new people have moved in. No, I don't see anyone of the old lot left.'

'You're forgetting Monsieur Crispin, Father,' interrupted the son, who was still standing on the threshold.

'Yes, that's true, but we don't see anything of him any more. I'm surprised he's still with us. He's been in a wheelchair for five years. He has two rooms on the fifth floor and the concierge takes him his meals and does his housework.'

'Was he friendly with the Antoine couple?'

'Let me think. There comes a time when you get things mixed up. He moved in a little after them. So Monsieur de Caramé was still alive. No, I don't think they saw much of each other. It was later, after Madame de Caramé had married Monsieur Antoine, that I used to see him talking to the husband. Because he was in commerce too, upholstery I think, he worked in Rue du Sentier.'

'Many thanks, Monsieur Caille.'

By now Janvier had arrived.

'Have you had any lunch?'

'I had a snack. What about you?'

'I'll have something to eat with Lapointe. Can you go up to the first floor and stay inside the apartment? Don't touch anything, even the smallest little trinket. You'll see why presently. Oh, there's just one person allowed in if she turns up, the niece.'

Ten minutes later, Maigret and Lapointe were at a table in the Brasserie Dauphine.

'A little aperitif?' the owner suggested.

'No, we'll have a carafe of Beaujolais straight away. What's on the menu?'

'Andouillettes, fresh in from Auvergne this morning.'

And for a starter, Maigret chose pickled herring fillet.

'So what do you think?' he began in a rather subdued voice.

Lapointe did not know what to answer.

'I'd never have believed what she said was true. I could have sworn that she was imagining things, because old people often do.'

'And now she's dead.'

'If her door hadn't been left ajar, it might have been days before anyone found her. She must have known the murderer, otherwise he wouldn't have needed to kill her.'

'I just wonder what he was looking for.'

'When we find that out, if we ever do, the investigation will be almost over. After lunch, we're going to examine her apartment inch by inch. There must have been something the murderer wanted to get his hands on. And something that was hard to find, since he had searched the place several times before.'

'But what if he's already found whatever he was looking for?'

'In that case, we'd have little chance of catching him. We'll need to question the other tenants. How many floors are there?'

'Six, plus the attics.'

'Two apartments on average on every level . . .'

The Beaujolais was perfect, and the andouillette, served with chips, was no less delicious.

'There's something I don't understand. Madame Antoine was eighty-six years old. She'd been widowed for twelve years. Why is it only now that someone got the idea of searching her apartment? Perhaps whatever it is had been in her possession only a short time? In which case, she should have known about it. But she told you she had no idea what it could be.'

'She seemed as much in the dark as us.'

'Neither of her two husbands was particularly mysterious. Not in the least. They were both absolutely average Frenchmen, one more imposing than the other.'

He signalled to the owner.

'Two coffees, Léon.'

The sky was just as blue as before, the air just as fresh. On the embankments of the Seine, tourists could be seen, cameras draped round their necks.

The two men returned to Quai de la Mégisserie. Now there was only one reporter loitering in the courtyard.

'I don't suppose you've got anything to tell me?' he muttered bitterly.

'No, nothing for now.'

'A lady went up there ten minutes ago, but she wouldn't say who she was.'

Soon afterwards, Maigret and Lapointe met the person he meant: a mannish-looking woman, who could have been between forty-five and fifty. She was installed in one of the armchairs in the sitting room and Janvier did not seem to have attempted to make conversation.

'You're Inspector Maigret?'

'That's correct. Allow me to introduce my two colleagues.'

'My name is Angèle Louette.'

'Madame?'

'No, it's Mademoiselle. I have a son of twenty-five, but I'm not ashamed of that, on the contrary.'

'And Madame Antoine was your aunt?'

'She was my mother's sister. Older sister. But it was my mother who died first, about ten years ago now.'

'And you live with your son?'

'No, I live on my own. I have a small place on Rue Saint-André-des-Arts.'

'And your son?'

'He lives here and there. I believe he's on the Côte d'Azur at the moment. He's a musician.'

'When did you last see your aunt?'

'About three weeks ago.'

'Did you visit her often?'

'About once a month, or perhaps every other month.'

'And did you get on with her?'

'Well, we never quarrelled.'

'What does that mean?'

'That we weren't really close. My aunt was a suspicious person. I'm pretty sure she thought I only came to see her so as to keep on good terms, and then inherit from her.'

'She had money?'

'She had some savings, certainly, though they can't have amounted to a very big sum.'

'Do you know if she had a bank account?'

'She never mentioned one to me. What she did keep telling me was that she wanted to be buried in the same grave as her first husband, who had a concession in Montparnasse Cemetery.

'Really, if she married again, I think it was so as not to be all alone. She was still young. She met Uncle Antoine somewhere, I don't know where. Then one fine day, she announced that she was getting married again, and asked me to be a witness.'

Maigret wasn't missing a word of what she was saying and he had signalled to Lapointe, who had taken his pad out, not to write anything down. She was the kind of woman who would probably have clammed up if they had put her through an official interrogation.

'Tell me, Mademoiselle Louette, did your aunt have any reason to fear for her life?'

'Not to my knowledge.'

'She never mentioned to you a mysterious visitor?'

'No, never.'

'Did she ever telephone you or come to see you?'

'No. It was me who'd come over now and then, to make sure she was all right and see if she needed anything. I was a bit anxious about her living alone. Anything could have happened and nobody would have known.'

'She didn't think of getting someone to help her in the house?'

'She could well have afforded it, because her two pensions were generous enough. I kept pressing her not to live alone, but she wouldn't even agree to have a cleaning lady. You can see how she kept this apartment. Not a speck of dust.'

'You're a masseuse, I believe?'

'Yes. I have a good clientele. I can't complain.'

'And your son's father?'

'He left me before the child was born. Which suited me, because he was a big mistake. It was just a passing infatuation, as people say. I've no idea what's become of him, and I probably wouldn't recognize him in the street.'

'So your son is registered as "father unknown", and he has your surname?'

'Yes, that's correct, his name is Émile Louette. But since

he's been playing the guitar in nightclubs, he's taken to calling himself Billy.'

'Are you on good terms with him?'

'He comes to see me now and then, usually when he needs money. He's very bohemian, but a good boy at heart.'

'Did he ever visit his aunt?'

'He used to come with me when he was little. But since the age of fifteen or sixteen, I don't think he's seen her.'

'Might he have asked her for money too?'

'That wouldn't be like him. Yes, he asks me, because I'm his mother, but he wouldn't go to anyone else, he'd be too proud.'

'Do you know this apartment well?'

'Yes, pretty well.'

'Where did your aunt sit when she was here?'

'In that armchair by the window.'

'How did she spend her days and evenings?'

'Well, she'd do the cleaning first, then go shopping. After that, she'd set about preparing her food, because she wasn't the sort of person to lunch off a scrap of cold meat on a corner of the kitchen table. She might have been all alone, but she ate proper meals in the dining room and she always laid a tablecloth.'

'Did she go out much?'

'If it was fine, she'd go and sit on a park bench.'

'To read a book?'

'No. She had trouble with her eyesight and said it was tiring to read. She just watched the passers-by, the children playing in front of her. She nearly always had a smile on her face, a slightly sad one. She was probably thinking of the past.'

'She didn't confide in you about anything?'

'What would there have been to tell me? She led a very simple life.'

'Did she have friends, women she might see?'

'All her old friends were dead and she didn't care to make new ones. Oh, I've just remembered, that was why she changed from her usual bench.'

'When was that?'

'Last summer, but towards the end of summer. She always used to sit on the same bench in the Tuileries Gardens. Then, one day, she saw a woman about her own age who asked her if the place beside her was free. She couldn't very well refuse. You can't save places on public benches. And from the first day, this woman started talking, telling her all about herself, how she was Russian in origin and had been a famous dancer.

'Next day, my aunt found her sitting in the same place, and this woman she didn't know talked to her for an hour about all her old successes. How she'd been in Nice for years. She didn't stop for a moment, complaining about the climate in Paris.

'This was one of the rare events my aunt actually told me about.

' "I was so fond of my bench," she would sigh. "I had to change not only the bench, but the part of the gardens I went to, or she'd have come along and sat by me again." '

'And did this Russian woman ever come here?'

'Not to my knowledge. And knowing my aunt, she would certainly never have invited her.'

'So, all in all, you have no idea who could have murdered her?'

'No, none at all, inspector. What should I do about the funeral?'

'Leave me your telephone number and I'll keep you informed. By the way, do you have any recent photographs of your aunt?'

'The last must be from over twelve years ago, because Uncle Antoine took it. It's better if you phone me in the evening because during the day I'm usually out seeing my clients.'

There was still a uniformed policeman standing at the street door.

'What do you think of her, chief?'

'She's willing to talk and seems pretty certain about everything.'

Janvier was looking around the room, wide-eyed.

'Is the whole apartment in the same style?'

'Yes, the bedroom's even more old-fashioned. Lapointe! Since you already know something about the building, can you go and knock on every door? Ask people if they ever met the old lady, how they got on with her, whether they saw her receive any visitors.'

In the sitting room, there was only one modern piece of furniture, a television set, placed opposite an armchair with a chintz cover.

'And now,' Maigret said to Janvier, 'we're going to go

41

through this place methodically, noting where every-thing is. It was because she found that her things had been slightly moved that she began to worry.'

The parquet floor, in which gaps had opened up over the years, was not covered by a carpet but by several rugs, one of them under the three legs of the round table.

They lifted the table and pulled up the rug to make sure nothing was hidden there. They then replaced the table, which was covered with a sort of lacy cloth. They took care to put the objects from it back in their correct place: a large seashell with *Dieppe* written on it, a china shep-herdess, and a pseudo-bronze statuette of a schoolboy, satchel on his back, dressed in a sailor suit.

On the mantelpiece, a series of photographs was lined up, showing two men, the two husbands presumably, who had perhaps merged in the old lady's mind. One of them was bald-headed and clean-shaven, with a plump, almost corpulent face, and had chosen to take up an imposing stance for the camera. That must be the one with an import-ant post with the Paris City Council.

The other, looking more modest, had a greying mous-tache. He was the kind of man you see all the time in the Métro or on the bus. He could have been a clerk, a civil servant, a foreman or a salesman in a department store, which was in fact the case. This one was smiling, and the smile was sincere. You sensed that he was a man content with life.

'By the way, Janvier. How did the niece get in? Did she have a front-door key?'

'No, she rang the bell and I opened the door.'

'This desk is locked. There must be some keys somewhere.'

He looked first in the old lady's handbag, the white leather bag she must have taken out of her wardrobe for the first days of spring. It contained no lipstick, just a compact of slightly blue-tinged face powder. An embroidered handkerchief bore the initial L, and they were soon to find that Madame Antoine's first name was Léontine.

No cigarettes. Obviously she didn't smoke. A little bag of violet-flavoured lozenges, bought on Rue de Rivoli. They must have been there a long time, as the sweets had stuck to each other.

'Here are the keys.'

He'd been almost certain he would find them in the handbag that she always had with her. There were three furniture keys, another that could be a bedroom key, and the one for the front door.

'She must have turned the key and put it back in her bag before she pushed the door open. Otherwise the keys would have been left in the lock or we'd have found them on the floor. She had just had time to put her bag on the chair before she was attacked.'

Maigret was talking more or less to himself, automatically, rather than to Inspector Janvier. He could not rid himself of a certain uncomfortable feeling. But even if he had come here the day before, what difference would it have made? He would not have found enough signs to justify sending someone to watch the apartment round the clock. And the murderer, being unaware of his visit, would have acted as he did, yesterday afternoon.

He tried the keys one after another in the drawer of the desk, and finally found the right one.

The drawer was full of papers and photographs. On the right, a savings book in the name of Léontine Antoine, Quai de la Mégisserie, totalling some ten thousand francs. It registered only deposits, no withdrawals, and the deposits had begun twenty-five years earlier. Which explained why the name Antoine had been written above the name de Caramé, which was crossed out.

Twenty-five years of a life, of savings. Shopping every morning. The park bench in the afternoon or perhaps, if it was raining, the cinema.

Another book contained records of a bank account at a branch of the Société Générale. Here the total was twenty-three thousand two hundred francs. Two thousand five hundred francs had been taken out shortly before Christmas.

'That sum doesn't ring a bell?'

Janvier shook his head.

'The television set. I bet she decided to spend the two thousand five hundred francs on that. She gave herself a Christmas present.'

There had been another withdrawal, twelve years earlier, no doubt for the funeral expenses of her second husband.

Some postcards. The largest number were signed Jean, and came from towns all over France, Belgium and Switzerland; they must have been sent whenever her husband attended a conference. The message was always the same: 'Affectionately, Jean.'

Jean was Monsieur de Caramé. Antoine had had little occasion to travel alone, and there were no postcards from him. On the other hand, there were plenty of photographs, of him on his own, or of the couple. The camera, which was quite a sophisticated one, was in the same drawer.

It looked as if the Antoines as a couple had gone to a different place every year for their holidays, and they liked making trips. They had been to Quimper, La Baule, Arcachon and Biarritz. They had travelled in the Massif Central and stayed on the Côte d'Azur. The photographs showed them at different ages, and it would have been possible to compose a chronological record of them.

There were a few letters there as well, mostly from the niece who was a masseuse, Angèle Louette. They too were from addresses in the provinces.

'Émile and I are enjoying our holidays here. Émile is a big boy now and spends his days playing in the sand dunes.'

There was just one photograph of this Émile who was now calling himself Billy. He was about fifteen and looking straight ahead with an air of defiance against the whole world.

'No secrets. Nothing unexpected,' Maigret sighed.

On a small table were some pencils, a penholder, an eraser and some unheaded writing paper. The aged Léontine could not have written many letters. Who would she have written to?

She had outlived the people she had known, they had all died before her. The only ones left were the niece and the great-nephew, of whom, apart from one photograph and a mention in an old letter from his mother, there was no trace.

They went meticulously through everything in the kitchen, and Maigret noticed various implements unfamiliar to him which did not seem to have been shop-bought. For instance, there was a cleverly designed tin-opener, and a simple but ingenious device for peeling potatoes.

They understood why when, after crossing the corridor, they opened a little room with the second key. This was outside the apartment proper, and was not much more than a large cupboard, with a window overlooking the courtyard. It contained a workbench and the walls were covered with tools, all hung up in perfect order.

So it was here that Antoine indulged his passion for making things. In one corner, on a plank, were piles of technical magazines and a drawer contained notebooks with sketches of devices, including one of the potato-peeler.

How many people were there like him, or couples like this, among the millions of Parisians? Small-scale, orderly, well-organized lives.

What was incongruous was the death of the frail little old lady with such pale grey eyes.

'We've just got the bedroom left now and the cupboards.'

The wardrobe contained nothing more than an astrakhan winter coat, another black woollen one, two warm dresses, one of them mauve, and a few summer frocks.

There were no men's clothes. When her second husband had died, she must have got rid of his things, unless she had access to one of the attic rooms on the sixth floor or some storage space in a loft. He would have to ask the concierge.

Everything was clean and neat and the drawers were lined with white paper.

But in the drawer of the bedside table, they noticed a rather large patch of grease or oil, although the drawer was empty.

Maigret, intrigued, sniffed at it, and had Janvier sniff it too.

'What do you think it is?'

'Grease of some sort.'

'Yes, but not just any kind of grease. This has been used to oil a gun. The old lady must have had a revolver or an automatic in this drawer.'

'So what's happened to it?'

'We didn't find it in the apartment, although we've searched everywhere. But this stain looks fairly fresh. Perhaps the person who killed the old lady . . .'

It was difficult to believe, though, that the murderer, whether man or woman, would have thought to take away the revolver.

This stain, discovered at the very last minute, completely altered the complexion of the case.

Had the old lady bought a gun in order to defend herself if she had to? It seemed improbable. As Maigret remembered her, she looked as if firearms would terrify her. And he found it hard to imagine her going into a gunsmith's shop, asking for a pistol, and trying it out in their basement.

But why not, after all? Had he not been surprised by her

energy? She was frail, with wrists no thicker than a child's, but she kept her apartment in apple-pie order, as well as or even better than the most house-proud of women.

'It probably belonged to one of the husbands.'

'But what's become of it now? Can you get this paper to the lab for them to analyse the grease? But I'm sure of the reply in advance.'

They heard a bell ring and, in spite of himself, Maigret looked round for a telephone.

'It's the doorbell,' Janvier said.

He opened the door to an exhausted Lapointe.

'You've visited all the tenants?'

'All the ones who were in. The worst of it was they'd hardly let me ask them questions, they kept asking *me*. How did she die? What kind of weapon was it? Why didn't we hear shots?'

'Any results?'

'In the apartment just above this one is a bachelor of about sixty, who's apparently a quite well-known historian. I saw his books on the shelves. He doesn't go out much. He has a little dog, and a housekeeper comes in every morning to clean and cook his meals. I call her a housekeeper, because that was the word he used. I saw her. She's known as Mademoiselle Élise, and she's very dignified. His place is practically as old-fashioned as this one, but a little more elegant. At one point he said to me:

' "If only she hadn't bought that damned television set! She has it on almost every night until about eleven. But I get up at six a.m. for my morning walk." '

And Lapointe added:

'He's never spoken to her. He's lived here for twenty years. When they met on the stairs, he would just nod to her. He remembers the husband, because he made a lot of noise too. Apparently there's a workshop here with lots of machine tools and in the evening you could hear him hammering, drilling, sawing, all sorts.'

'And the apartment opposite him?'

'There was nobody in. I went downstairs to ask the concierge. They're a young couple. The man is a sound engineer for a film company and his wife a film editor in the same firm. They usually eat out in the evenings and get home late. They get up late too, because they only start work at midday.'

'And the third floor?'

Lapointe consulted his notes.

'Family called Lapin. I only saw the grandmother and the baby. The wife works in a clothes shop on Rue de Rivoli and the husband's in insurance. He travels a lot.'

'And the other apartment?'

'Just a minute. I questioned the grandmother, and she said: ' "No monsieur, I didn't have anything to do with her. That woman was too immoral for me. If you want to know why, just look at her, with her two husbands. I'm a widow too. Did I get married again? Did I go on living in the same apartment, with the same furniture, with another man?" '

Lapointe returned to his notebook.

'Father Raymond. Not sure what order he belongs to. Very old and practically never leaves his flat. He didn't even recognize the name of Léontine Antoine, ex-Léontine de Caramé.

'Moving on to the next floor up: there's one empty apartment, which is being renovated for people to move into in two weeks: repainted and generally made as good as new. A couple aged about forty with school-age children.

'I saw the old man that the concierge does for. He's in a wheelchair which he manages with extraordinary skill. I thought I'd find a bitter old fellow, tired of life, but on the contrary he was full of good humour.

' "Oh," he said, "she's been killed, has she? Nothing's happened in this building for fifty years or more. And now we have a juicy murder on our hands. Do they know who did it? I suppose it can't have been a crime of passion." '

Lapointe added:

'That made him laugh. He was really cheerful. If he'd been able to get downstairs, he'd probably have asked us if he could visit the crime scene.

'There's a woman living opposite him, Madame Blanche, about sixty, works as cashier in a bar. I didn't see her, because she only gets home at midnight.'

A small world, everyone living cheek by jowl. The old woman on the first floor had been murdered, and it had created little stir. Only:

'Who killed her?'

'How did they do it?'

'Why didn't she call out?'

Most of them had vaguely greeted her on the stairs, but without speaking to her. Everyone had been in his or her own little retreat, behind closed doors.

'Stay here until I send someone to relieve you,' Maigret

told Janvier. 'It may sound silly, but I think the man or woman who was searching this apartment might come back.'

'Send Torrence if he's free. He loves watching television.'

Maigret took with him the paper with the grease stain. At Quai des Orfèvres, he went straight upstairs to Moers' laboratory.

'Can you examine this stain for me?'

Moers sniffed at it, looked at Maigret as if to say, this won't be difficult, and took the paper over to one of the specialists in the huge room under a sloping roof.

'Just as I thought. Gun grease.'

'I need an official analysis, because this is the only clue we have so far. Has it been there long?'

'My man will tell you that, but he needs more time.'

'Thank you. Have the results sent to me.'

He went downstairs to his office and then into the inspectors' room. Torrence was there with Lapointe, who was already writing up his notes.

'Torrence, tell me. Are you hungry?'

The bulky Torrence looked startled.

'At five in the afternoon?'

'You probably won't get a chance to eat later. Have a bite now, or pick up some sandwiches. You're going to 8a, Quai de la Mégisserie where you'll replace Janvier in an apartment on the first floor. I'll have you relieved early tomorrow morning. You'll find the keys on the round table in the sitting room.

'You'll need to be alert, because the murderer also has a key and didn't have to force the door.'

'You think he'll be back?'

'This case is so peculiar that anything's possible.'

Next, Maigret called Doctor Forniaux.

'Have you had time to do a post-mortem?'

'I was just going to dictate my report. Do you know, this woman, given her state of health, could have gone on to be a hundred! Her organs were in as good a condition as those of a young girl.

'She was smothered, as I thought from the start. I think it will have been with a scarf or something with red threads in it, because I found one between her teeth. She tried to bite it. She certainly put up a fight before she ran out of oxygen.'

'Thanks, doctor. I'll wait for your report.'

'You'll get it first thing tomorrow.'

Léontine Antoine didn't drink, since there had been no wine or alcohol in the apartment. She ate a lot of cheese. These were the details that occurred to Maigret as he watched the traffic on the Pont Saint-Michel. A convoy of barges was going under the bridge, pulled by a tug with a large white trefoil on its funnel.

The sky was pink, tinged with blue, the leaves on the trees were still a tender shade of green, and the birds were singing loudly.

It was just then that Picot, the officer who had first noticed the old lady, asked if the inspector would see him.

'I don't know if this interests you. I've just seen the photograph in the paper. That lady, I know her. What I mean is, I saw her nearly a week ago. I was on duty outside the main door. She wandered about on the pavement for a while, looking up at the windows and peeping into the courtyard. I thought she was going to speak to me, but she went off without saying anything.

'She came back next day and this time she was bold enough to step inside the courtyard. I didn't stop her. I just thought she was a tourist, because there are plenty of them. The day after that, I wasn't on duty. Lecoeur was replacing me, and he saw her go inside and take the stairs up to the Police Judiciaire. He didn't ask if she had a summons, because she seemed so determined.'

'Thank you. Put it in a report. And Lecoeur the same.'

So it seemed she had been haunting police headquarters for some time before asking to see Inspector Maigret. And he had sent her Lapointe, whom she had at first taken for his son.

Which had not prevented her, after that, from waiting for him on the pavement.

Old Joseph was knocking at his door, as was his habit, and opened it without waiting for an answer.

He held out a form, on which the name written was *Billy Louette*.

Yet the masseuse had told Maigret a few hours earlier that she thought her son was somewhere on the Côte d'Azur.

'Show him in, Joseph.'

3.

'I suppose you've been looking for me?'

'Not yet. Your mother said you were on the Côte d'Azur.'

'Oh, what my mother says, you know! . . . Is it all right to smoke?'

'If you wish.'

The young man did not seem overawed to be inside police headquarters and apparently considered Maigret to be simply an official of no particular rank.

This was neither defiance nor ostentation on his part. His ginger hair was rather long, but he did not look like a hippy. He was wearing a suede jacket over a checked shirt, with beige corduroy trousers and moccasins.

'When I read in the papers what had happened to my aunt, I thought right away you'd want to see me.'

'I'm glad you've come.'

He did not in the least resemble the masseuse. Whereas she was tall and heavily built, with man-sized shoulders, he was short and quite thin, with bright blue eyes. Maigret had sat down behind his desk and motioned to him to take the armchair opposite.

'Thank you. So what exactly happened to the old lady? The papers didn't say much.'

'They say what we know: she was murdered.'

'Was anything stolen?'

'Apparently not.'

'In any case, she didn't keep much cash at home.'

'How do you know?'

'Because I'd go and see her now and then.'

'When you were short of money?'

'Yes, of course. Otherwise, what was I going to talk to her about? My life wouldn't interest her.'

'And she gave you some?'

'Usually a hundred-franc note, but I wasn't supposed to come back too often.'

'You're a musician, I gather?'

'Yes, I'm a guitarist, I play in a group called Les Mauvais Garçons.'

'And can you make a living doing that?'

'We have our ups and downs. Sometimes we're hired to play in an important nightclub, other times we play in cafés. What did my mother tell you about me?'

'Nothing very much.'

'Well, as you can see, she's not exactly overflowing with motherly affection. For a start, we've very little in common. My mother thinks only about money, about how she's going to fare in her old age, as she says, so she saves all her pennies. She'd go without eating if she could, so as to have more to put away.'

'Was she fond of your aunt?'

'She couldn't stand her. I've often heard her say with a sigh: "When's the old bird going to hop the twig?"'

'Why did she want to see her dead?'

'Well, to inherit, of course! With two pensions, the old lady must have had some pretty substantial savings. But

I liked her a lot, and I think she liked me too. She'd always insist on making me coffee and bringing out the biscuits. She'd say: "I'm sure you don't get enough to eat every day. Why don't you learn a proper trade?"

'My mother wanted me to learn a trade too. She even picked out something for me when I was fifteen: she wanted me to be a chiropodist. She'd say: "There are so few of them you have to wait a week for an appointment. Now that's an occupation that pays well and it's not unpleasant."'

'When did you last see your great-aunt?'

'About three weeks ago. We'd hitchhiked to London, hoping to get some work, but the groups over there are better than us, they play in all kinds of combinations. We came back stony broke, so I went round to see her.'

'And she gave you your hundred francs.'

'Yes, and some biscuits.'

'Where do you live?'

'I move around a bit. Sometimes I'm shacked up with a girl and other times I live on my own. Which I'm doing at the moment. I'm renting a room in a small hotel in Rue Mouffetard.'

'And you have work?'

'Up to a point. You know the Bongo Club?'

Maigret shook his head. The young man seemed surprised that anyone might not have heard of the Bongo Club.

'It's a little café-restaurant on Place Maubert. The owner's from the Auvergne. He caught on very quickly to the kind of neighbourhood it is. So there's quite a hippy clientele, and he sometimes allows drinks on the house.

And in exchange for a free dinner and a few francs, he also has live music performers, which is where we come in. We do our set twice or three times in the evening. And there's a girl called Line, a fantastic singer. That brings him customers. They come along to stare at the famous hippies, and they don't believe us when we say we don't smoke marijuana or hash.'

'Do you intend to carry on being a musician?'

'Yes. I hope so. That's all that matters to me. I've started writing songs too, but I haven't found my voice yet. But what I can tell you is that I didn't kill the old lady. In the first place, that's not me, I don't go round killing people. But in any case, I'd be sure to be suspected right away.'

'Did you have a key to her apartment.'

'What would I have done with one?'

'Where were you yesterday at about six p.m.?'

'In bed.'

'Alone?'

'Well, I was by then. We'd been up almost all night at the Bongo. I'd picked up a girl who seemed nice: a Scandinavian type, Danish or Swedish. We had a lot to drink. I took her home with me in the early morning, and it must have been three in the afternoon before I went to sleep. Later on, I realized she'd got out of bed, and I heard her moving about. I didn't wake up properly, but I sensed there wasn't anyone beside me any longer.

'I was really hung over, and absolutely worn out, so I didn't get up myself until after nine o'clock.'

'So in other words, nobody can vouch for you between, let's say, five and eight p.m.?'

'That's correct.'

'Might you be able to find this girl again?'

'If she isn't at the Bongo tonight, she'll be in some other club in the neighbourhood.'

'You know her well?'

'No.'

'So she's a new girlfriend?'

'It's not the way you think it is. We come and go. I told you we went to London. We hitchhiked to Copenhagen too, and everywhere we go, we pick up new friends.'

'Do you know her name?'

'Just her first name: Hilda. And I know her father is quite a high-up civil servant.'

'How old is she?'

'Twenty-two, she told me, I don't know who she was going to meet, otherwise she might have stayed with me for weeks. That's the way it goes. You split up, half the time you don't know why, but you stay friends.'

'Tell me about your relations with your mother.'

'I already told you we don't get on.'

'But she brought you up.'

'She didn't really want to, and that's one of the reasons she didn't like the old lady. She'd hoped my aunt would look after me. Because my mother went out to work, she had to take me to the crèche every morning and fetch me in the evening. Same thing when I started school. She didn't like having a kid, and it was a nuisance when she had men around.'

'Did she often have men around?'

'It depended. Once we lived for six months with this

guy I was supposed to call papa, and he was usually hanging about the house.'

'He didn't go out to work?'

'He claimed to be a sales rep, but he didn't seem to get out much. Other times, I might hear sounds in the night, but next morning there would be nobody there. The men were nearly always younger than her, especially as time went on.

'About a fortnight ago, I met her on Boulevard Saint-Germain with this tall skinny guy I've quite often seen round the clubs. People call him "Big Marcel".'

'You know him?'

'Not personally, but the word is he's a pimp. And she likes a drink, don't forget.'

He was both cynical and candid.

'But look, I don't suspect my mother of killing my aunt. My mother's just the way she is. So am I, and I wouldn't be able to change either. Perhaps I'll make it big time, and perhaps I'll just end up another no-hoper like all the others in Saint-Germain-des-Prés. Got any more questions for me?'

'Plenty probably, but I can't think of any just now. Are you happy with your life?'

'Most of the time, yes.'

'You wouldn't prefer to have become a chiropodist like your mother wanted? You might be married with children yourself by now.'

'It doesn't tempt me. Maybe later.'

'What effect did it have on you when you read that your great-aunt was dead?'

'My heart did miss a beat. I didn't know her all that well. As far as I was concerned, she was this very old woman who by rights ought to have died years ago. But I liked her all the same. I liked her eyes and the way she smiled.

' "Eat up," she'd say to me. And she'd watch me munching my biscuits with this kind of tender look. Apart from my mother, I was all the family she had.

'She'd say: "Come on, why don't you get your hair cut?" That was what bothered her most. She'd go: "It makes you look like what you're not. Because basically, you're a good boy." '

'So when's the funeral?'

'I don't know yet. Leave me your address and I'll see you're informed, probably in the next couple of days. But it depends on the examining magistrate.'

'Do you think she suffered?'

'She put up a bit of a fight, not much. Do you have a red woollen scarf or one with a red pattern?'

'I never wear a scarf. Why do you ask?'

'No reason, I'm just searching. We're feeling our way.'

'And you don't suspect anyone?'

'No one in particular, no.'

'Could it have been a burglary?'

'But why choose Madame Antoine and attack her in a building that's crammed with people? The murderer was looking for something.'

'Money?'

'I'm not sure about that. If he knew her, he must have been aware that she only kept very small sums of money at home. And anyway, this person had visited her apartment several times when she wasn't there. Do you know if she owned any valuables?'

'She had a few jewels, but nothing very grand. Just modest bits of jewellery she'd received from her two husbands.'

Maigret had found them: a ring with a garnet, and matching earrings. A gold bracelet and a small gold watch.

In the same box, there had been a pearl-topped tie-pin which must have belonged to Caramé, and some silver cuff-links. All of these were very old-fashioned and with practically no sale value.

'Did she have any documents?'

'What do you mean, documents? She was a very simple old woman who'd lived a peaceful life, first with husband number one, then later with the second one. I never knew Caramé, he died before I was born, but I knew the other one, Joseph Antoine. He was a good sort.'

Maigret stood up with a sigh.

'Do you often visit your mother?'

'Hardly ever.'

'Then you don't know whether she is on her own or whether this Marcel character you mentioned is living with her?'

'You're right, I've no idea.'

'Thank you for coming in, Monsieur Louette. Perhaps one of these days I'll turn up to hear you play.'

'The best time for that is eleven p.m.'

'By then, I'm usually in bed.'

'Am I still a suspect?'

'Until we have evidence to the contrary, everyone's a suspect, but you're no more so than anyone else.'

Maigret closed the door after the young man and went to rest his elbows on the window-sill. Dusk was falling. Outlines were less clear. He had learned a great many things, but they were of no use to him.

What on earth could someone be looking for in the home of the old woman on Quai de la Mégisserie?

She'd lived for over forty years in the same apartment. Her first husband had had nothing mysterious about him, then she had lived on as a widow for about ten years.

And the second husband did not seem to have anything out of the usual about him either. He had died years ago, and since then she had led a monotonous existence, without seeing anyone except her niece and great-nephew.

But why had no one tried to get into her apartment before this? Did it mean that whatever they were looking for had not been there long?

He gave a shrug, sighed and headed for the inspectors' office.

'See you tomorrow, boys.'

He went home by bus, reflecting that he had a strange job. He looked round at his anonymous fellow passengers, telling himself that at an hour's notice, he might have to investigate the life of one of them.

He had found the red-headed boy with long hair likeable enough, whereas now he felt moved to ask his mother some indiscreet questions.

Madame Maigret opened the door when he reached their landing, as always.

'You look preoccupied.'

'No wonder. I'm struggling with a case that I don't understand at all.'

'The old lady who was murdered?'

She had read the newspaper, of course, and listened to the radio.

'You met her when she was alive?'

'Yes.'

'What did you think of her?'

'I told myself she was mad, or a bit touched anyway. She was a tiny slip of a thing, very fragile, and she begged me to take up her case, as if I was the only person in the world who could help her.'

'And did you do anything?'

'I couldn't provide her with round-the-clock police protection. All she was complaining about was that sometimes, when she got home, she would find that objects weren't in their usual place.

'I'll admit I thought she was imagining things, or perhaps her memory was failing. But I did promise myself I'd call round to see her, more to reassure her than for any other reason. Yesterday, she must have come back sooner than usual from her walk, and the visitor, man or woman, was still in the apartment.

'All that person had to do was press a scarf or some other piece of material over her face to smother her.'

'Did she have any family?'

'Just a niece and a great-nephew. I've seen both of them. The niece is massive, built like a man – she actually works as a masseuse. The young man, on the contrary, is small and skinny. He has red hair and plays the guitar in some club in Place Maubert.'

'And nothing was stolen?'

'It's impossible to tell. The only clue, if we can call it that, is that there had been a revolver in the drawer of her bedside table, and it's no longer there.'

'You wouldn't kill an old woman in cold blood for the sake of a revolver. And you wouldn't search an apartment several times for it either.'

'Let's eat.'

They dined, just the two of them, by the open window, without switching on the television. It was a very mild evening. The air stood still, as a pleasant coolness took hold; they could faintly hear the leaves quivering on the trees.

'Since you didn't come home at midday, I've warmed up the lamb stew for now.'

'Good idea.'

He ate with appetite, but his mind was elsewhere. He could still see the little old lady in grey on the pavement of Quai des Orfèvres and the lively gaze of trust and admiration that she had turned on him.

'Can you try not to think about it any more this evening?'

'I wish I could. I just can't help it. I hate letting people down, and what's happened now is that the poor old woman has lost her life.'

'Would you like to go for a walk?'

He said yes. He had no desire to stay all evening inside the apartment. And also, during an investigation, he had a habit – some might call it an obsession – of repeating the same actions every day.

They walked down towards Bastille where they sat at a café terrace. A long-haired guitarist was playing, as he made his way between the tables, while a girl with dark-rimmed eyes held out a saucer to the customers.

That, of course, made him think of the red-haired great-nephew, who probably went round the cafés busking when he was short of cash.

Maigret gave more generously than usual, as his wife noticed. She said nothing, simply smiled, and they spent a little while staring ahead at the lights in the darkness.

He was smoking his pipe slowly with short puffs. For a moment, he was tempted to go to the Bongo Club. But what would be the point? What more could he learn there than he knew already?

The other tenants in the building on Quai de la Mégis-serie had to be suspects too. Any one of them might have known the old lady better than they admitted. It would be easy enough to make an impression of her front-door lock and have a duplicate key made.

But why? That was the question that kept returning to Maigret's mind. Why?

In the first place, why had there been all those previous visits? Not for the small sum of money kept in the apartment: only a few hundred francs, and easy to find in the desk drawer. But they hadn't been touched. Maigret had found the banknotes slipped inside a savings book.

'Tomorrow I'll start investigating the two husbands.'

It seemed ridiculous – especially since the second one had now been dead for twelve years.

There must be a secret somewhere, a secret important enough to have caused the sacrifice of a human life.

'Shall we go on walking?'

He had drunk a small glass of calvados and had been on the point of ordering another. That would not have pleased his friend Doctor Pardon, who'd warned him off all alcoholic drinks.

'You can tolerate wine and spirits for years, but there comes a time when the organism can't take them any more.'

He shrugged his shoulders and made his way out through the tables. On the pavement, Madame Maigret linked arms with him. Boulevard Beaumarchais. Rue Servan. Then Boulevard Richard-Lenoir and their good old apartment.

Contrary to his fears, he fell asleep almost at once.

Nothing happened at Quai de la Mégisserie overnight, and the bulky Torrence was able to sleep as much as he wished in the old lady's armchair. At eight in the morning, Lourtie had gone to relieve him and found a reporter having an animated conversation with the concierge.

It was a grumpy and heavy-footed Maigret who pushed open the door to the inspectors' office at nine, and signalled to Janvier and Lapointe to follow him.

'And you can come too, Lucas.'

He sat at his desk and chose a pipe as if this selection was very important.

'Now then, boys. We're no further forward than we were yesterday morning. So for lack of any clues in the present, we're going to explore the past. Lucas, you go to the Bazar de l'Hôtel de Ville, to the department where they sell tools and gardening implements. Some of the salesmen who were just starting out when Uncle Antoine worked there must still be in their jobs.

'Ask them anything you like. I want to know everything about him, his character, his way of life, that kind of thing.'

'Understood, chief. But should I get permission from the management? They won't dare refuse, and the people working there will be more at ease than if I went to talk to them in some unofficial way.'

'Very well. Janvier, you go to the City Council offices and do the same for Caramé. It'll be more difficult, because it's a long time now since he died. If the only people who would remember him have retired, get their addresses and visit them at home.'

Routine steps, of course, but sometimes routine pays off.

'And as for you, Lapointe, you're coming with me.'

In the courtyard, the young inspector asked:

'Shall we take a car?'

'No. We're only going to the other side of the bridge, Rue Saint-André-des-Arts. It would take longer in a car.'

The building was old, like the house in Quai de la Mégisserie, and indeed all the buildings in the neighbourhood. On one side was a picture-framer's, on the other a cake shop. The glass-panelled door of the concierge's lodge opened on to a corridor leading to a courtyard.

Maigret went into the lodge and gave his name. The concierge was a plump, rosy-cheeked little woman who must have had dimples in her cheeks as a child, and they were still there when she smiled.

'I thought we might be getting a visit from the police.'

'Why?'

'When I read what had happened to that poor old lady, I thought right away that one of my tenants here was her niece.'

'You mean Angèle Louette?'

'Yes.'

'Did she ever mention her aunt to you?'

'She doesn't chat much as a rule, but now and then she stops and passes the time of day with me. We were talking once about people who didn't pay the rent and she said some of her customers were like that, and she didn't like to insist because they were important people. "But luckily, one day, I'll inherit from my aunt!" She said it just like that. She told me her aunt had had two husbands, so she collected two pensions, and she must have had plenty of money put by.'

'Does she receive many visitors?'

The concierge looked embarrassed.

'What do you mean?'

'Well, do other women, friends, sometimes come to see her?'

'Friends? No.'

'Or customers?'

'She doesn't work here, she goes to people's homes.'

'Does she have male visitors?'

'Oh well, after all, why shouldn't I say so? Yes, some-times. One of them stayed here about six months. He was at least ten years younger than her, and he did the shop-ping and housework.'

'Is she home at the moment?'

'She went out about an hour ago, because she starts her rounds early. But there's someone upstairs.'

'One of her usual visitors?'

'I don't know. She got in rather late last night. When I released the catch, I heard the footsteps of two people. But I didn't see anyone come back down.'

'Does that happen often?'

'Not that often, just from time to time.'

'What about her son?'

'He's hardly ever here. I haven't seen him for months. He looks a bit of a hippy, but I think he's a nice enough boy.'

'Thank you. We'll just take a look upstairs.'

There was no lift. The apartment faced on to the court-yard. The door was not locked and Maigret went in, followed by Lapointe, to find himself in a living room with modern furniture in department-store style.

Hearing no sound, he pushed open a door. Lying in the double bed was a man who opened his eyes and stared at them with a startled expression.

'What is it? What do you want with me?'

'I wanted to see Angèle Louette, but since you're here . . .'

'Aren't you . . . ?'

'Inspector Maigret, yes. And we've already met, a long time ago. You were a barman in Rue Fontaine in those days. People used to call you "Big Marcel".'

69

'They still call me that. Do you mind? I need a minute to find my trousers, I haven't got anything on.'

'Go right ahead.'

He was indeed tall, with a thin and bony body. He quickly slipped on his trousers and searched for his slippers under the bed.

'You know, Angèle and me, it's not what you think. We're good friends. We spent the evening together, and I didn't feel well. So instead of traipsing all the way across Paris to my place, Boulevard des Batignolles . . .'

'Of course. And just by chance, you happened to find your bedroom slippers here.'

Maigret opened a wardrobe. Hanging inside were two men's suits, along with some shirts, socks and underwear.

'All right. Now, let's hear what you have to say.'

'Can I get myself a cup of coffee?'

Maigret followed him into the kitchen where Big Marcel set about preparing his coffee, as if well used to doing so.

'There's nothing to say. I've had some ups and downs, as you well know. I've never been a pimp, though, like some people have tried to make out. And the police have always had to let me go.'

'How old are you?'

'Thirty-five.'

'And her?'

'I don't rightly know. She must be getting on for fifty. Maybe she already is.'

'Big romance, is it?'

'We're just good friends. She can't manage without me.

If I don't show up here for a week or so, she comes looking for me in all my usual haunts.'

'Where were you, late afternoon, the day before yesterday?'

'The day before yesterday? Let me think. I can't have been far from here, because I was supposed to meet Angèle at seven.'

'She didn't mention it.'

'She won't have bothered. We were supposed to be going for a meal. I sat with my aperitif on the terrace of a café on Boulevard Saint-Germain.'

'And she arrived at seven?'

'She may have been a bit late. Yes, now I think of it, she was very late. One of her ladies had kept her waiting. She turned up at about seven thirty in the end.'

'And you had dinner together as arranged?'

'Yes. Then we went to the cinema. The restaurant's called Chez Lucio, Quai de la Tournelle, they know me well there.'

'And what is your occupation at present?'

'Well, tell you the truth, I'm looking for work, but it's not so easy at the moment.'

'So you're a kept man?'

'You're really trying to hurt my feelings, aren't you? Just because, years ago now, the police tried to pin stuff on me. Yes, all right, she's lent me some money now and then. But she doesn't earn a lot herself.'

'Were you going to sleep here all morning?'

'She should be back soon, because she's got a gap between appointments. She went to see you yesterday, and she told you everything she knew. So what are you doing here today?'

'Well, it's given me a chance to meet you again, hasn't it?'

'Can you go into the living room and let me take a shower?'

'I'll even give you permission to have a shave while you're about it,' said Maigret with irony.

Lapointe was astonished at what they had just heard.

'Yes, he's been arrested four or five times, accused of pimping. And he was suspected of being an informer for a Corsican gang that was active in Paris a few years ago. But he's a slippery customer, and we've never been able to prove anything about him.'

Footsteps could be heard on the stairs. The door opened. Madame Antoine's niece stood stock still on the threshold.

'Come on in. I've just dropped by to pay you a little visit.'

She glanced anxiously at the bedroom door.

'He's in there, yes. He's just having a shower and then a shave.'

She finally closed the door with a shrug.

'Well, all this is my own business, isn't it?'

'Possibly.'

'Why do you say possibly?'

'It so happens that he's an old acquaintance of mine, and his activities in the past were not looked on too favourably by the law.'

'Do you mean he's a thief?'

'No, not to my knowledge. But when he was a barman, there were two or three women working for him in the neighbourhood, including one who was, let's say, a hostess in the same establishment.'

'I don't believe you. Anyway, if that was true, he'd have gone to prison.'

'No, you're right, he didn't go to prison. Because there wasn't enough evidence.'

'That still doesn't tell me why you are here.'

'Let me ask you a question first. Yesterday, when you mentioned your son, you said he was on the Côte d'Azur.'

'I told you that was what I thought.'

'In reality, he hasn't left Paris and we had a very interesting chat.'

'I know he isn't fond of me.'

'He's as fond of you as you were of your aunt, you mean?'

'I don't know what he's been telling you. He's a hothead. He'll never amount to anything.'

'The day your aunt died, you had a date for seven o'clock with Big Marcel in a café on Boulevard Saint-Germain.'

'If he told you so, that's because it's true.'

'And what time did you arrive?'

This seemed to unsettle her a bit, and she hesitated for a while before replying:

'One of my ladies kept me waiting. It must have been about seven thirty when I got there.'

'Where did you eat dinner?'

'In an Italian restaurant, Quai de la Tournelle. Chez Lucio, it's called.'

'And after that?'

'We went to the cinema at Saint-Michel.'

'Do you know what time it was when your aunt was murdered?'

'No, I only know what you've told me.'

'It was between half past five and seven o'clock.'

'What difference does that make?'

'Do you own a gun?'

'Certainly not. I wouldn't know how to use one.'

Marcel emerged from the bedroom, freshly shaved, wearing a white shirt and tying a blue silk tie.

'You see?' he said in a jocular tone. 'These gentlemen woke me up. There they were, standing at the end of the bed. I wondered if I was in a film!'

'Do *you* own a revolver?' Maigret asked him.

'Not likely! That's a quick way to get nabbed.'

'Which number on Boulevard des Batignolles do you live?'

'Number 27.'

'Thank you both for your cooperation. Regarding your aunt, mademoiselle, you may have the body fetched from the Forensic Institute and arrange the funeral any day you wish.'

'Will I have to pay for it out of my own pocket?'

'That's your business. Since you're her closest relation, you'll inherit enough money to have some left after the funeral.'

'What do I have to do? Ask a lawyer?'

'Go the bank, they'll advise you. If you don't know already, you'll find her savings book and chequebook in a drawer of the desk.'

'Thank you.'

'Don't mention it. But don't forget to let me know the time of the funeral.'

He had rarely seen a gaze as stony as the eyes looking at him. As for Marcel, he was affecting a casual air.

'Good day to you, Monsieur Maigret,' he said ironically.

Maigret and Lapointe made their way downstairs, and at the next street corner, Maigret went into a bar.

'That pair made me feel thirsty. A beer, please. What'll you have?'

'The same.'

'Two, then.'

Maigret mopped his forehead with his handkerchief.

'And this is what we end up doing, when an old lady with grey eyes dies a violent death. You go to see people and ask them a lot of more or less silly questions. Those two up there must be laughing at us now.'

Lapointe did not dare say anything. He did not enjoy seeing the chief in this mood.

'Mind you, that happens in almost every investigation. There's a moment when the engine's turning over without connecting, you don't know where to go next. Then something happens, something quite minor, often, that you don't at first consider important.'

'Your good health, chief.'

'Yours.'

It was still morning. The street was cheerful with housewives doing their shopping. They were not far from Rue de Buci street market, which Maigret particularly liked.

'Come along.'

'Where are we going now?'

'Back to base. See if Lucas and Janvier have had more luck.'

Janvier had returned, but not Lucas.

'It was easy, chief. The man who took over from Caramé still works for the Council, and he knew him well from the days when he started there.'

'Tell me.'

'Nothing to hide, except that behind his back they called him "His Majesty Caramé". He was a man who had a certain style and attached great importance to his appearance. He was proud of his position as well, and was hoping to get the Légion d'honneur as he'd been promised. He took every chance to wear a formal suit, because he looked good in it. His brother was a colonel in the army.'

'Still alive?'

'No, he was killed in Indochina. Caramé talked about him a lot. He used to say, "My brother the colonel . . ." '

'And that's all?'

'All they could tell me. No known vices. But he regretted not having a child. An old doorman told me a story about him, but there's no guarantee it's true. Apparently, after three or four years of marriage, he sent his wife to a gynaecologist, but the doctor asked to see her husband. In other words, it wasn't her that couldn't have children, it was him. After that, there was no more talk of offspring.'

Maigret was pacing up and down in the office, still looking irritable. Now and then, he stopped at the window, as if asking the Seine to bear witness to his bad luck.

A knock at the door. It was Lucas, who had run up the stairs and was out of breath.

'Take your time.'

'In the hardware department, I found someone who'd worked directly under Monsieur Antoine. He's sixty now, and a department head himself.'

'What did he say?'

'Seems Antoine was a kind of crank. In a good way. That is, he had his hobby. When people asked him what he did, he'd say: "I'm an inventor."'

'And it's true he'd been granted a patent for a special kind of tin-opener and sold it to a manufacturer of kitchen goods. And he'd invented other things too . . .'

'A potato-peeler, by any chance?'

'How did you know?'

'Saw it in the apartment on Quai de la Mégisserie.'

'He was always trying to perfect his inventions. It seems he had a workshop at home and spent all his spare time in it.'

'Yes, I saw that too. Did he invent anything more important?'

'Not as far as the man I talked to knew, but apparently he would sometimes nod at you with a secretive air and say: "One of these days I'll make a real discovery, and everyone will be talking about me."'

'Nothing more precise?'

'No. Apart from his obsession, he was a man of few words, but he did his job conscientiously. Didn't drink. Didn't go out in the evening. Seemed happy enough with his wife. I say happy, but not in love, well, given their ages . . . They got on well, they respected each other. This man had been round for dinner a couple of times at Quai de la Mégisserie, and he thought they seemed cosily settled there.

' "A charming woman," he said. "So refined! The only thing that was a bit odd was that when she was speaking, you didn't know whether she was referring to her first husband or the second. It was as if she mixed them up.'

'And that's all?'

'Yes, chief, that's all.'

'Well, we have one detail for certain: there was, not long ago, a gun in the drawer of the bedside table. And this gun's disappeared. I think I'll just go over to Boulevard des Batignolles. Coming, Lapointe? Get one of the cars, not the one that keeps stalling.'

Before leaving the office, he picked out a different pipe.

4.

The artificial marble plaque outside the door of the small hotel announced: *Furnished rooms, by the day, the week or the month. All mod cons.*

Most of the tenants rented by the month, and the mod cons consisted of a washbasin in each bedroom and a bathroom on every other landing.

To the right of the entrance was a reception desk with pigeon-holes for mail and keys hanging on the wall.

'Is Big Marcel in?'

'Monsieur Marcel? He just came in. His car's outside.'

It was a bright red convertible, though the model dated back quite a few years. Two little boys were nevertheless staring at it with envy, guessing how fast it would go.

'Has he lived here long?'

'Over a year. Very good tenant.'

'But he doesn't often stay overnight, if I'm not mistaken.'

'He usually comes home in the early morning, because he works at night. He's a barman in a nightclub.'

'Does he bring women back here?'

'Not often. None of my business, anyway.'

The owner was a fat man, with two or three unshaven chins, and he wore shabby bedroom slippers.

'Which floor?'

'Second. Room 23. I hope you're not going to cause trouble. I know who you are! And I don't much like seeing the police in the building.'

'Well, you're properly registered, aren't you?'

'With you people, you never know.'

Maigret went upstairs, followed by Lapointe. A printed notice at the foot of the staircase said: *Please wipe your feet* and a handwritten message underneath read: *No cooking in the bedrooms*.

Maigret had seen this before. It didn't stop the tenants all having a little spirit stove, to warm up the ready-made meals they could buy from the nearest charcuterie.

He knocked at Room 23, heard footsteps, and the door opened abruptly.

'Well, well!' said Marcel in mock surprise. 'Here already, are we?'

'Were you expecting us?'

'When the police stick their noses in one place, you can be pretty sure they'll be turning up again.'

'Were you going to move out?'

There was a suitcase on the bed and another on the floor. The ex-barman had been putting clothes in them.

'Yes. I'm clearing out. I've had enough.'

'Enough of what?'

'Enough of that female, who ought to have been in the army.'

'Have you quarrelled?'

'Yes, we had a bit of a row. She called me all kinds of names, because I was still in bed when you came round.

I'm not a masseur. I don't go to people's houses and pound their flesh for them.'

'That doesn't explain why you're changing your hotel.'

'I'm not just changing my hotel, I'm off, and I'm going to Toulon. Got some pals there, real ones, they'll find me a job.'

Maigret recognized in one of the cases the blue suit he had seen earlier hanging in the wardrobe in Rue Saint-André-des-Arts. As for the other suit, Marcel was wearing it. His name was in fact Montrond, but no one ever used it, and the hotel owner too had referred to him as Monsieur Marcel.

'The red car outside, that's yours?'

'Yes, not worth much. Ten years old. But she can still put on a turn of speed.'

'You'll be leaving by road, then?'

'Exactly. Unless you've taken it into your head to stop me.'

'Why would we stop you?'

'Because, with the cops, you never know where you are.'

'I've got a question for you. Have you ever been to the apartment on Quai de la Mégisserie?'

'Why would I go there? To pay my respects to the old lady? "Good morning madame. I'm your niece's lover. Seeing as I'm in a spot of bother just now, she's been keeping me, because she always needs a man around. She's a real cow, let me tell you, and you don't want to promise her too much."'

He went on packing his bags, looking round for anything he might have forgotten in a drawer. He took a camera out of one of them. There was a record player as well.

'There we are! I'm just waiting for you to go, and I'll be off.'

'Is there an address where we can reach you in Toulon?'

'You can always write to me at the Amiral Bar, Quai de Stalingrad. Care of Bob, the barman, an old pal. Do you think you'll be needing me again?'

'Like you said, you never know.'

Before the suitcases were closed, Maigret felt around inside them, but found nothing suspicious.

'How much money did you get from her?'

'From that gendarme? Five hundred francs. And even then I had to promise her I'd be back soon. You never know what she's after. Sometimes she treats me like dirt and kicks me out. Then a few minutes later, she's weeping and wailing and saying she can't live without me.'

'Bon voyage,' said Maigret with a sigh, making for the door.

As he passed reception, he said to the owner:

'Looks like you're losing one of your tenants.'

'Yes, he told me. He's going down south and he'll be away a few weeks.'

'Will you keep his room for him?'

'No, but we'll give him another.'

The two men returned to headquarters. Maigret put a call through to Toulon.

'I want to speak to Chief Inspector Marella. This is Maigret at the Police Judiciaire.'

He immediately recognized his colleague's voice. They had started in the police together and now Marella was in charge of the Police Judiciaire in Toulon.

'How are you?'

'Can't complain.'

'Do you know a bar called the Amiral?'

'You bet I do. Hangout of all the bad boys in town.'

'Fellow called Bob?'

'The barman. He acts as their letterbox.'

'Tonight or tomorrow, a certain Marcel Montrond will be turning up in Toulon. He'll probably go straight to the Amiral. I'd like you to keep an eye on him.'

'What do you suspect him of?'

'Everything and nothing. I don't know, really. He seems to be mixed up in a case we're getting nowhere with.'

'Is this the old lady on Quai de la Mégisserie?'

'That's right.'

'Odd business, eh? Of course, I only know what's been in the papers and on the radio, but it sounds a bit of a damned mystery. Have you clapped eyes on the boy with the guitar?'

'Yes. It doesn't look as if he's involved. But then it doesn't look as if anyone's involved, and there doesn't seem to be any obvious reason why the old lady was killed.'

'I'll keep you in the picture. This Marcel you're talking about, he wouldn't be known as Big Marcel, would he?'

'The same.'

'Bit of a gigolo, isn't he? He's been down on the Côte d'Azur more than once and every visit, he seems to pick up an older woman to play up to.'

'Thanks, I'll be in touch.'

The telephone rang almost immediately.

'Inspector Maigret?'

'Yes.'

'This is Angèle Louette. First, I wanted to tell you I've sent that good-for-nothing packing . . .'

'Yes, I know, he's on his way to Toulon.'

'Believe me, he's really not my type, and he won't take me in again like that.'

'Why, what's wrong with him?'

'He lives off women and he lounges about half the day in a bed that doesn't even belong to him. He didn't want to go, I had to give him money before he would.'

'I know.'

'Did he brag about it?'

'Yes, of course. He calls you "the gendarme", by the way.'

'I was also going to tell you the funeral will be tomorrow morning. The coffin will be brought round to Quai de la Mégisserie. We won't have a ceremonial wake, because my aunt didn't know anyone. The funeral will be at ten.'

'It's in church?'

'There'll be a committal in Notre-Dame-des-Blancs-Manteaux. You still haven't found anything?'

'No.'

'Have you got my son's address?'

'Yes, he gave it me.'

'I'd like to be able to get in touch with him. Because he might want to come to his great-aunt's funeral, in spite of everything.'

'He's living at the Hôtel des Îles et du Bon Pasteur, Rue Mouffetard.'

'Thank you.'

Maigret was well aware of the impatience of examining magistrates, and a little later he went through the door separating the Police Judiciaire from the Palais de Justice.

In the corridors lined with magistrates' offices, there were clients, witnesses, or persons under arrest on almost all the benches, and some of those waiting between two gendarmes were in handcuffs.

Examining Magistrate Libart was alone with his clerk.

'Well now, inspector, where are we with this case?'

He sounded almost cheerful as he rubbed his hands together.

'I wanted to let you work in peace. But are you getting anywhere yet?'

'Not at all.'

'No suspect?'

'No really credible suspect, no. And not a single clue, except that the murderer was surprised by the old lady while he was looking for something in her apartment.'

'Money?'

'No, I don't think so.'

'Jewels?'

'He'd have got hardly anything for the ones she owned.'

'A madman, then?'

'That's unlikely. Why would a madman pick on her apartment? And why go there several times before the afternoon when the crime was committed?'

'Someone within the family? Someone in a hurry to inherit?'

'That's possible, but not very probable. The only heir

would be her niece, who is a masseuse and seems to earn her living reasonably well.'

'You seem discouraged.'

Maigret forced himself to smile.

'I'm sorry. It's a difficult time to get through. The funeral's tomorrow.'

'Will you go?'

'Yes, that's been my long-term practice and it's often given me a lead.'

He returned home for lunch and Madame Maigret, seeing his preoccupied expression, avoided asking him any questions.

She was almost walking on tiptoe and had made fricandeau of veal with sorrel sauce, one of his favourite dishes.

When he was back at Quai des Orfèvres, Lapointe knocked at his office door.

'Come in.'

'Excuse me, chief. What should I be doing?'

'Nothing. Whatever you like . . . If you've got any ideas . . .'

'I thought I might go back to the bird-seller. He sees people coming in and out of the building. Perhaps if I press him, he'll remember something.'

'Yes, if you like.'

Maigret hated feeling like this, without any inspiration or imagination. The same thoughts kept coming back to him, but they led nowhere.

First, Madame Antoine was not mad.

Why then had she been walking up and down outside

headquarters before she dared to contact the police? Did she suspect someone?

She had realized that they would just shrug their shoulders if she complained about seeing her things being moved around.

And yet it was quite true. Someone had been searching her apartment several times.

But what were they looking for?

As he had told the magistrate, it couldn't have been money. Or jewellery either.

Yet it had been sufficiently important for the mysterious visitor to murder the old lady when he was surprised in the act.

Had the intruder finally found what he or she was after? And then been leaving with the booty, just at the moment she returned, earlier than usual?

What could a very old lady, twice widowed and living modestly, possibly own that would be worth killing her for?

He scribbled some vague doodles on a piece of paper and suddenly became aware that they looked a bit like the old woman.

At about five o'clock, he started to feel stifled in his office and set off for Quai de la Mégisserie. With him he had a photograph of Big Marcel, which he had found in the archives of the Vice Squad.

It was a poor likeness, the features more strongly marked than in reality, but still, it was recognizable. He started with the concierge.

'Have you ever seen this man?'

She had to go and fetch her glasses from the sideboard.

'I don't rightly know. His face seems a bit familiar. But there are plenty of people just like him.'

'Take a good look. It would have been quite recently, if at all.'

'It's the checked suit that strikes me. I think I've seen the same kind of suit a week or two back, but I can't say where.'

'Here, in your lodge?'

'No, I don't think so.'

'In the yard? On the stairs?'

'Honestly, I don't know. Your inspector was round asking me questions just now. I'm not going to make things up. Did you know that she's been brought back here?'

'Madame Antoine?'

'Yes, her niece is up there. She's left the door open and put candles either side of the bed. A few of the tenants have ventured in and said a little prayer. If I could find anyone to take over for me, I'd go to the funeral tomorrow, but I'm on my own here. My husband's been in a psychiatric ward for three years now.'

Maigret was back on the pavement, in front of the birdcages. The younger Caille recognized him at once.

'Well, now! I've just had one of your inspectors here, the young one.'

'Yes, I know. Can you take a good look at this photo?'

He looked at it, shook his head, examined it again closely, then from a distance.

'Can't say I recognize him, but it reminds me of something.'

'His suit?'

'No, not particularly. The expression on his face. It's kind of mocking.'

'Not one of your customers?'

'No, certainly not.'

'Could you ask your father?'

'I will, but he doesn't see too well.'

When he came back he shook his head again.

'No, he doesn't recognize him. But then my father's nearly always inside and he's only interested in his birds and his fish. He's so fond of them he doesn't really want to sell them.'

Maigret went back into the building and up to the first floor. The woman living opposite Madame Antoine's apartment was just coming out, a shopping bag in her hand.

'She's in there,' she whispered, pointing to the open door.

'Yes. I know.'

'They're burying her tomorrow. Seems her first husband had a concession in Montparnasse Cemetery, and she wanted to be buried there alongside him.'

'Who did she say that to?'

'Her niece, I suppose. And the concierge. She said Ivry was too far away, she'd feel lost among all the thousands of graves.'

'I want to show you something. May I come in for a minute?'

This apartment was neat and tidy, darker than the old lady's, because a tree outside blocked light from the windows.

'Have you ever seen this man?'

And he once more brought out the little photo from police archives.

'Should I recognize him?'

'I don't know. That's what I'm asking you.'

'Well, if you're asking whether I've seen him before, then yes I have. Not so long ago. He was smoking a cigarette. I wondered what was missing from the snap – a cigarette.'

'Take your time. Think about it.'

'It wasn't one of the tradesmen. Nor someone I saw in the courtyard either.'

He felt she was doing her best.

'I suppose this is important?'

'Yes.'

'To do with Madame Antoine?'

'Probably.'

'But if I gave evidence, it would harm him, wouldn't it?'

'Quite possibly.'

'So you see why I can't be too certain. I wouldn't want to harm an innocent man.'

'If he is innocent, we'll find out.'

'It doesn't always happen! There are miscarriages of justice. Oh all right, it was when I was going out . . .'

'Which day?'

'I couldn't say. But last week. I was on my way to pick up my daughter from school.'

The girl, aged about twelve, was sitting doing her homework in the next room.

'So it must have been a little after four, then.'

'Or it could have been at midday. That's what I'm trying

to remember. More likely four o'clock, because I had my shopping bag, and that's when I buy food for the evening. My husband doesn't come home for lunch, so we don't eat much at midday, me and my daughter.

'I was on the stairs, not looking where I was going, and someone bumped into me. He was rushing up the stairs four at a time and nearly knocked me over. That's why I remember it.

'He turned back and asked me if he had hurt me. I said no, it was all right.'

'You don't know which floor he was going to?'

'No, I was in a hurry because my daughter doesn't like me to keep her waiting outside the school and, with the traffic, I don't dare let her come back on her own.'

Maigret sighed. A slight hope, at last!

A few moments later, he was pushing open the door of the bedroom where the open coffin lay, and was able to gaze at the fine features of the old woman whom everyone had supposed to be mad.

The curtains were three-quarters drawn and the bedroom was in semi-darkness, except for a quivering ray of sunlight. The two church candles flickering either side of the bed helped to give the room an unaccustomed appearance.

Angèle Louette was there, neither moving nor speaking, in an armchair, and for a moment Maigret thought she was asleep. Only on looking at her for the second time did he notice that her dark eyes were fixed on him.

He stood respectfully for a moment in front of the dead woman, then went into the sitting room where he was relieved to be in the light of day. As he expected, she followed him.

She was more stony-faced than ever.

'What are you doing here?'

'Paying my last respects to your aunt.'

'Oh, admit it, that's the least of your concerns. Same thing for the tenants here. Just two of them, out of all the people in the building, have been in. Have you seen that waste of space, Marcel?'

'He's gone to Toulon in his car.'

He could see that this came as a shock to her.

'Good riddance! It was hard enough to get him out of the door. Did you know I had to give him five hundred francs before he'd leave my place?'

'You could report him to the police for extorting money.'

'Well, maybe I will. Anyway, if he tries to come back—'

'Did you know that he was in this building last week?'

She gave a violent start and frowned.

'Do you know which day?'

'No.'

'Or what time?'

'About four o'clock.'

'Did he tell you that?'

'No.'

'And you asked him about this visit?'

'When I saw him this morning, I wasn't aware of it. How would he know your aunt's address?'

'One day, oh about a month ago, we were crossing the Pont-Neuf together, and I pointed out her windows and said:

' "I've got an old aunt who lives up there." '

'I think you must have added that one of these days she'd leave you a tidy sum of money.'

'I can see he's been spinning you his lies. I only said that she'd been married twice, so what with her pensions, she was very comfortably off. Where is he now?'

'At this moment, as I said, unless he's changed his mind, he's on the way to Toulon.'

'He was always going on to me about Toulon and his friends there.'

'Do you know anything about his family, his background?'

'No.'

'He never told you anything about his past?'

'No. All I know is he's still got his mother. She lives in a small town somewhere in central France.'

'Are you certain you haven't set foot in here in the last week, or let's say the last fortnight?'

'Are you going to start this again?'

'Think before you reply.'

'I'm certain.'

'Do you know what was in the drawer in her bedside table?'

'No, I've never opened it.'

'Even this morning, when you were rearranging the furniture for the coffin to be brought in?'

'Even this morning.'

'Did you know that your aunt owned a gun?'

'Certainly not. She'd be the last person to pick up a firearm.'

'She wasn't afraid, living on her own?'

'My aunt wasn't afraid of anything or anybody.'

'Did she ever tell you about her second husband's inventions?'

'One day, she showed me some clever little device for peeling potatoes. She even promised me one, but I never got it. That was when Antoine was still alive. She gave me a tour of his workshop as well, if you can call it that, more like a cupboard with hardly room to turn round.'

'Well, thank you for your time.'

'Are you coming to the funeral?'

'Yes, probably.'

'The coffin will leave here at a quarter to ten. We have to be at the church by ten.'

'Till tomorrow then.'

There were moments when her quasi-masculine toughness was not unattractive and could be seen as sincerity. She wasn't beautiful, had never been pretty. And as she got older, she was starting to put on weight.

Why shouldn't she, like any unmarried man of her age, have the right to carry on affairs?

She didn't conceal it. She received her lovers at her apartment overnight or for a week. The concierge saw them coming and going. The other tenants in her building must know about them too.

On the other hand, she was distrustful, and kept looking at him as if she was always suspecting a trap.

On the way back to headquarters, Maigret stopped off at the Brasserie Dauphine to drink a glass of white wine from the Loire valley. He didn't want a beer. The wine, which had a touch of sparkle about it, misted the glass and suited the spring atmosphere better.

It was an in-between time of day. Apart from a delivery-man in a blue apron, there was no one in the café.

He decided to order the same again.

Doctor Pardon wouldn't get to know about it. Anyway, Pardon had merely advised him to drink in moderation.

At Quai des Orfèvres, he found Lapointe, who had once more been round the apartment building, showing tenants the photo of Marcel.

'Any success?'

'No.'

'Tomorrow I'll need you to drive me to the funeral.'

He went home on foot, with thoughts that were on the whole uncomfortable rumbling round inside his head:

'The only thing we're sure of is that a revolver has disappeared.'

And were they even sure of that? They had found some grease from a gun at the bottom of a drawer. But perhaps there was some other explanation for that.

Moers' experts had assured him that it had been there no more than a month.

He was starting to feel suspicious of everything himself, and he would have liked to start the investigation again from scratch, if only he had a clue to put him on the right track.

'Oh, you're back already!'

She hadn't opened the door, and for once he had used his key.

'I think I'll go out this evening.'

'Where to?'

'A place you'd best not come to, a hippy hangout on Place Maubert.'

He took the time to read his newspaper and had a cold shower before dinner. Once again, they were eating in front of an open window.

'Tomorrow I have to go to the funeral.'

'Will there be a lot of people?'

'Apart from the niece, I might be the only person there. Only two of the tenants in the building she lived in came to pay their respects in front of her coffin.'

'What about the press?'

'The case doesn't seem to have aroused much interest. Now all they're printing are a few lines on page three.'

He switched on the television. He would have to wait until after ten if he was to find Billy Louette at the Bongo Club.

On the corner of Boulevard Voltaire, he hailed a taxi, gave the address, and the driver looked at him with curiosity, wondering why a respectable gentleman from this district was going to a rather disreputable place.

The Bongo Club had taken few pains over the decoration. The walls were painted white, with occasional meaningless stripes of colour.

That was the only sign of originality. There was a classic zinc counter behind which the club's owner, in shirtsleeves and blue apron, was handling orders himself. A door gave on to a smoke-filled kitchen from which came a smell of stale cooking fat.

A dozen or so couples were eating at tables, mostly spaghetti, which seemed to be the speciality of the house.

Some of the young men wore jeans and flowered shirts. The others were people who had come along to watch.

Or rather to listen, since three musicians were making as much noise as an entire orchestra. Billy was the guitarist, and the other two were playing drums and bass.

All three of them had long hair and were wearing black velvet trousers and pink shirts.

'Are you here to eat?'

The owner practically had to shout to make himself heard.

Maigret shook his head and ordered a glass of white wine. Billy had seen him come in, without showing any sign of surprise.

Maigret knew nothing about rock music, but what was reaching his ears didn't sound any worse than the kind of thing he sometimes heard on the radio or television. The three young men were throwing themselves into it and working up into a sort of final frenzy.

People applauded loudly. The band took a break. Billy came over to Maigret, who was standing at the counter.

'I suppose it was me you wanted to see?'

'Yes, of course. Have you been in touch with your mother?'

'Not today, no.'

'In that case, you won't know that the funeral is tomorrow. You'll need to be at Quai de la Mégisserie at a quarter to ten. The service is at Notre-Dame-des-Blancs-Manteaux. Then she will be buried in Montparnasse Cemetery.'

'I thought my great-uncle Antoine was buried out at Ivry.'

'Quite right, but his widow expressed the wish to be buried in the vault belonging to her first husband.'

'We're going to be playing again in a few minutes. Did you like our stuff?'

'Unfortunately, I don't know anything about that kind of music. There was one question I wanted to ask you. Did you know that your great-aunt owned a revolver?'

'Yes.'

At last, someone was replying straightforwardly, without any sign of being worried.

'She told you about it?'

'A long time ago, could be a year or two. I was broke again. I went to ask her for some money and I saw that she had a few hundred-franc notes in her sideboard. Well, to some people, a few hundred francs is nothing at all. But I know others, and that includes me at times, who'd think it a fortune. So I said quite naturally to her:

' "Aren't you afraid?"

' "Who of? You?"

' "No, but you live alone. People know that. A burglar might . . ." '

At this point he made a sign to his fellow musicians that he wouldn't be long.

'And she said she was armed against burglars, and went to open the drawer in her bedside table.

' "And don't think I wouldn't use it if I had to," she said.'

So now they had more to go on than a mere patch of oil. Someone had actually seen the gun.

'Was it a revolver or an automatic?'

'What's the difference?'

'A revolver has a barrel, an automatic is flat and snub-nosed.'

'Well, if I'm remembering it right, it was a revolver.'

'How big?'

'Oh, I don't know, I didn't look closely. About as long as my hand.'

'Did you tell anyone about it?'

'No, no one.'

'You didn't say anything to your mother?'

'Our relationship isn't close enough for me to confide in her about anything.'

The young man went off to join his companions, and the music started again. You could sense that Billy was really carried away by the rhythm he was creating, backed up by the drummer.

'He's a good boy,' the owner said, leaning across the bar. 'Well, the three of them are OK, and they don't take drugs. Which is more than I can say of all my customers.'

Maigret paid for his drink and went back outside. He had difficulty finding a taxi, and asked to be driven straight home.

Next morning, he went up to the next floor to see Libart, the examining magistrate.

'I'd like you to authorize a search warrant. In the name of Angèle Louette, unmarried, who works as a masseuse, and lives in Rue Saint-André-des-Arts.'

The clerk was writing this down.

'Does this mean you're getting close to a result?'

'I've no idea. I'll admit that I'm still pretty much in the dark.'

'She's the old lady's niece, isn't she?'

'That's right.'

'And her legatee as well. Seems a bit odd, in that case.'

Maigret was expecting this objection, which had occurred to everyone. Angèle Louette was certain to inherit from her aunt one day, and probably quite soon, given the old lady's age. So why would she risk spending the rest of her life in prison to get her hands on what would in any case have come to her?

'Well, follow your hunch! Good luck.'

At a quarter to ten, Maigret was at Quai de la Mégisserie, with Lapointe, who was driving the little black police car. There were no funeral drapes round the front door, and no crowd had gathered, not a single curious onlooker.

The hearse pulled up in front of the building, and two burly men went up to fetch the coffin. There were no flowers or wreaths. Curtains twitched at some of the windows, and the concierge came to the door and crossed herself.

The old bird-seller left the dark interior of the shop for a few minutes to join his son at the entrance.

And that was all.

Angèle Louette was alone as she climbed into the black limousine provided by the undertaker. The church was empty apart from two women waiting outside a confessional. It was as if everyone was in a hurry to get it over with, the priest as well as the undertaker's men.

Maigret had remained at the back of the church where Lapointe joined him after finding a parking spot.

'It doesn't even feel sad,' the young inspector remarked.

That was true: the nave was flooded with sunlight. The doors had not been closed and the sounds of the street could be heard.

'*Et ne nos inducas in tentationem . . .*'

'*Amen . . .*'

The men carried out the coffin, which could not have weighed much. Less than a quarter of an hour later, they were entering Montparnasse Cemetery, and the cortège stopped in front of a pink marble tombstone.

'I told you there wouldn't be anyone here,' the masseuse whispered to him as the old lady's coffin was lowered into the vault.

She added: 'We haven't had time yet to have her name engraved on the stone, alongside her husband's. The monumental masons will do it next week.'

She was dressed soberly, all in black, which made her look even more severe. She could have been taken for a governess or a headmistress.

'And now,' murmured Maigret, 'we're going over to your place.'

'*We're* going?'

'Yes, that's what I said.'

'What is it you want with me now?'

The cemetery was even more cheerful than the church, with bright sunlight dancing in the leaves on the trees and the air full of birdsong.

'Wait a minute. I'd better give the undertaker's men tips. I suppose I can't go back in their car?'

'There's room in ours.'

They met up again at the gates and Angèle got in the back, while Maigret took his usual place alongside Lapointe.

'Rue Saint-André-des-Arts.'

The old lady's niece said bitterly:

'I was expecting there'd be talk. There are always people who'll say things behind your back, making things up if they have to. But for the Police Judiciaire, and Detective Chief Inspector Maigret in person, to harass me . . .'

'I'm sorry about this, but I'm just doing my job.'

'But why would I have gone secretly to my aunt's?'

'Why would anyone else?'

'Do you think I'm capable of killing an old woman?'

'I don't think anything, I'm just carrying out an investigation. Lapointe, you can come up and join us once you've parked.'

When they were upstairs, she took off her hat and then her suit jacket, under which she wore a white blouse. For the first time, Maigret noticed that although she had a rather masculine appearance, she had a good figure, remarkably well preserved for her age.

'Now, tell me once and for all what you want.'

He took the search warrant out of his pocket.

'Read it for yourself.'

'You mean you're going to turn everything upside down, poking in every corner?'

'Don't worry, we're used to this. I'm waiting for two specialists from Criminal Records, who will put everything back in its exact right place.'

'I don't believe this!'

'By the way, your son didn't come to the funeral.'

'I must admit that what with everything else going on, I forgot to tell him about it. I don't even know his precise address. All I know is what you've told me.'

'You may not have got in touch with him, but I did, and that's why I was surprised not to see him. He seems like a nice young man.'

'Well, as long as he gets his own way.'

'Such as not wanting to be a chiropodist.'

'He said that?'

'He's much more straightforward than you and I don't have to ask him the same question ten times.'

'If he'd had the life I have! You can do as you please, but I need a glass of something.'

She drank not wine, but whisky, taking it from the living-room sideboard, which held an assortment of bottles.

'Would you like some?'

'No.'

'Or wine? Red? White?'

'Nothing for now.'

The men from Criminal Records arrived before Lapointe, who was heaven knew where, still trying to find a parking spot.

'Here we are, boys. Go through all the rooms with a fine toothcomb. You know what we're looking for, but you might find something else of interest. All I ask is that you put everything back carefully in its place.'

She had lit a cigarette and sat down in an armchair by the window, from which there was a view of rooftops and a little corner of the Eiffel Tower.

'You can stay here with them,' he told Lapointe, who had finally arrived. 'I've got something else to do on this side of town.'

Once outside, he headed for Rue Mouffetard, but not without stopping for a glass of white wine in a bistro where there were boiled eggs on the counter.

5.

The hotel was a tall, narrow building, full of strong smells.
Maigret climbed to the fourth floor and knocked at the
door which had been indicated to him, with bad grace, at
reception.

A sleepy voice called out: 'Come in!'

The shutters were closed, and the room was dark.

'I thought it might be you.'

The red-haired youth jumped out of bed, quite naked,
and grabbed a towel, which he draped round his
hips. Still under the covers was a girl, turned towards
the wall, her dark hair lying across the pillow all one
could see.

'What's the time?'

'The funeral was over quite a while ago.'

'And you're wondering why I didn't turn up? Give me
a minute to rinse out my mouth. Terrible hangover.'

He filled a tooth mug at the washbasin and swilled out
his mouth.

'You should have stayed longer last night. These three
English guys turned up with guitars and we were jam-
ming for a couple of hours. They had a great chick with
them. Who's right here.

'I just couldn't force myself up this morning to go to
the old lady's funeral. Not very respectful of me, I know,

but I didn't all that much want to meet my mother. Has she found the loot?'

'What loot?'

'My great-aunt's savings. She must have plenty stashed away, because she spent hardly anything. Her second husband had some put by as well. So my mother will get her little house in the end.'

He opened the shutters, through which a ray of sunshine entered the room. The girl moaned and turned over, exposing one naked breast.

'Your mother wants to buy a house?'

'Yeah, a little house in the country for weekends, and then to retire to one day. She's been dreaming of it for years. She tried to get her aunt to lend her enough money, but that didn't come off. Sorry, I can't offer you anything here.'

'I was just passing.'

'And you still haven't found the revolver?'

'No. Big Marcel has left town.'

'Oh, no kidding! Well, my mother'll be in a state.'

'She threw him out herself. He's gone to Toulon, where he has friends.'

'She'll have to find someone else, then. She can't go three days without a man. As she gets older, it's getting harder and costing more.'

His cynicism wasn't aggressive. His tone seemed almost affectionate as if nostalgic for the kind of family life he had never really known. So he was laying it on a bit thick.

'Don't leave Paris without informing me. The investigation is far from over, and I might need you again.'

The young man jerked his chin towards the bed.

'As you can see, I've good reason to stay.'

Maigret returned to Rue Saint-André-des-Arts, where the men from Criminal Records were waiting for him.

'Finished now, chief. Practically nothing to report. Just clothes, mostly dark-coloured, underwear, stockings, shoes. She must have a weakness for shoes, we found eight pairs.'

Angèle Louette was still sitting in her chair, apparently indifferent.

'The fridge is well stocked. Although she lives alone, she cooks proper meals. There are photos too, of herself and a child, dating back to when she was young. And an account book, where she records her income and the names of her clients.'

'You're forgetting the main thing,' the other man interrupted.

The first man shrugged.

'Well, if it means anything. On top of the wardrobe, there's some dust, and in the dust, a patch of grease or oil. The kind you use for guns.'

Angèle intervened at this point.

'There's never been a gun in this house.'

'But the traces look recent, and there's a greasy piece of paper in the bin that could have been used to wrap up a revolver.'

'In that case, it must be Marcel who had one, and he's taken it away with him.'

Maigret climbed on to a chair to see the grease stain for himself.

'I'm summoning you to attend at Quai des Orfèvres at three this afternoon.'

'What about my clients? Do you think I don't have anything to do?'

'I'm going to issue you with an official summons.'

He took a yellow form from his pocket and filled in the blanks.

'Three o'clock, as I said.'

Lapointe was waiting patiently. They went back to the little black car parked about three hundred metres away. Moers' men had left as well.

'Does she have a telephone?'

'Yes.'

'She'll probably take advantage of being alone to call Toulon. Were there any photographs of the old lady there?'

'Three or four, but quite old. There's one of a man with a moustache. She told me that was Antoine.'

Maigret went home for lunch. His wife asked no more questions than the day before, except about the funeral.

'Were there many people there?'

'Apart from the niece, just Lapointe and me. The service was conducted at breakneck speed. You'd have thought everyone wanted to have done with her.'

When he returned to the office, Janvier told him:

'Chief Inspector Marella rang from Toulon and wants you to call him back.'

'Get him on the line, then.'

A few minutes later, he was put through.

'Marella?'

'Yes. I called you in case it's of interest. Your man Marcel got here quite late last night and headed straight for the Amiral. He recognized me, acknowledged me, and went over to sit at the counter. He and Bob were talking in low voices after that. I couldn't hear anything, because they had the jukebox playing at top volume.'

'Nobody else with them?'

'No. At one point, Bob went to the phone booth and called someone. When he got back, he was looking pleased and made a sign that I read as "everything's OK".'

'And that's all?'

'No. Your Marcel checked into a room in the Hôtel des Cinq Continents, Avenue de la République. He was up at nine a.m. and went off in the car to Sanary. Does that ring a bell?'

'No.'

'One of the Giovannis lives there. The older brother, Pepito.'

The Giovanni brothers had long been regarded as gangland bosses on the Côte d'Azur. The younger one, Marco, used to live in Marseille. Pepito had acquired a luxury villa at Sanary, where he was now leading a quiet life.

They had been arrested a dozen times, but it had always been difficult to make charges stick, for lack of evidence.

They were getting on in years now, and ending their days under the guise of wealthy pensioners.

'Did Marcel stay long at the villa?'

'Nearly an hour. He went back to the Amiral, then had lunch in an Italian restaurant in the old town.'

'Has he had any contact with the Giovannis before?'

'Not that I know of.'

'Can you have Pepito watched? I'd like to know if he makes any moves in the next few days, or receives visitors at the villa who aren't the usual callers.'

'I'll see to it. If you'll return the favour one day too. How's your case going?'

'Some leads seem to be materializing, but I'm still not getting anywhere. When it's all over, I think I'll come and recharge my batteries in the sun, somewhere in your neck of the woods.'

'It would be a pleasure. How long since we last saw each other?'

'Ten, twelve years? The Porquerolles affair, I think.'

'Yes, I remember. See you soon then, Maigret.'

They had started work together at Quai des Orfèvres and for over two years had pounded the streets, before being assigned first to the railway stations, then to the big department stores. They had both been young and unmarried in those days.

Old Joseph came in to hand him the summons he had issued to Angèle.

'Show her in.'

She looked paler and more tense than usual. Was she simply impressed by the atmosphere at the Police Judiciaire?

'Sit down.'

He pointed to an ordinary chair facing his desk, and opened the door into the inspectors' office.

'Could you come here, Lapointe? Bring your notebook.'

Young Lapointe, who often acted as his minute-taker, sat down at the end of the desk, pencil in hand.

'As you can see, this time you're being questioned officially. Anything you say will be taken down and you can sign the statement afterwards. I'll probably have to ask you some questions you've already answered, only this time, your answers will be recorded.'

'In short, you think I'm the number one suspect?'

'No, just *a* suspect, there aren't any numbers. You were not fond of your aunt.'

'All she did when I told her I was pregnant was give me a hundred-franc note.'

'So what you held against her was her avarice.'

'She was self-centred. She didn't give any thought to other people. I'm sure the reason she married again was for money.'

'Did she have a difficult childhood?'

'No, you couldn't even say that. Her father was a man of means, as they used to say. The family lived near the Luxembourg Gardens and the two daughters, my mother and my aunt, had a good education. It was only in his middle years that my grandfather began to speculate and lost all his money . . .'

'Was that when she married Caramé?'

'Yes. He used to visit my grandparents quite often. And they all thought for a long while it was to see my mother. I think she thought so too. But in the end, it was my aunt who hooked him.'

'What about your mother?'

'She married a man who worked in a bank, and was in delicate health. He died young, and my mother had to go to work in a shop in Rue de Paradis.'

'So you were brought up in modest circumstances?'

'That's right.'

'Your aunt didn't come to your assistance?'

'No. Then, I don't quite know why, I chose to train as a masseuse. Perhaps because there was one who lived in our building, and she had a car she drove to visit her clients.'

'You have a car too?'

'Just a little Citroën 2CV.'

'To drive to your house in the country when you get one?'

She frowned.

'Who said anything about that?'

'It doesn't matter. But apparently you've always dreamed of having a little house in the country, not too far from Paris, where you could go for weekends.'

'Well, I don't see what's wrong with that. Plenty of people have a dream like that, don't they? My mother certainly did, but she died before it ever came true.'

'How much do you hope to inherit from your aunt?'

'Forty or fifty thousand francs. I don't know the exact figure. I'm going by the kind of thing she let drop now and then. Though she may have had other assets.'

'So what it amounts to is that if you went on visiting her, it was simply because of the inheritance?'

'If you want to put it like that. She was after all my only living relation. Have you ever lived alone, Monsieur Maigret?'

'What about your son?'

'I hardly ever see him, just when he's short of money. He doesn't have any affection for me.'

'Think carefully before replying to my next question and don't forget that your answers are being written down. Did you often go to your aunt's house when she wasn't there?'

He had the impression that she turned paler, but she did not lose her composure.

'Is it all right if I smoke?'

'Go ahead, but I haven't got any cigarettes to offer you.'

On his desk there were only pipes, six of them arranged in order of size.

'I asked you a question.'

'Could you repeat it?'

He did so at once.

'It depends what you mean. There were days when I might arrive at Quai de la Mégisserie before she got home. And in that case, I'd wait for her.'

'Inside the apartment?'

'No, on the landing.'

'Might that be for a long time?'

'If she was late back, I'd sometimes take a walk along the embankment. Or I especially liked looking at the birds in the shop downstairs.'

'Your aunt never considered letting you have a key to her apartment?'

'No.'

'What if she had been taken ill suddenly?'

'She was convinced that would never happen to her. She had never fainted in her life.'

'And the door was never left open?'

'No.'

'Even when she was there?'

'No, she locked it behind her.'

'Who was she suspicious of?'

'Everyone.'

'Including you?'

'I don't know.'

'Did she show you any affection?'

'She never showed any kind of emotion towards me. She would tell me to sit down. She'd make me coffee and fetch biscuits from the tin.'

'And she didn't ask you for news of your son?'

'No. She must have seen him about as often as she saw me, more perhaps.'

'Did she ever mention cutting you out of the inheritance?'

'Why would she do that?'

'I'd like to get back to the locked door. The lock, and I checked it, wasn't complicated. It would be easy enough to take an impression.'

'What for?'

'Never mind. I'll ask you again, putting it a little differently. Have you *ever*, even once, found yourself alone in her apartment?'

'No.'

'You've thought carefully about that?'

'Yes.'

'Your aunt might have gone out while you were there, just to the shops, if she found she didn't have any biscuits left, for instance.'

'No, that never happened.'

'So you would never have had occasion to look inside any of the drawers?'

'No.'

'Have you ever seen her savings book?'

'I saw it one day when she took something out of the desk, but I don't know how much was in it.'

'And her bank book?'

'I've no idea what she had in the bank. To tell the truth, I didn't even know she had a bank account.'

'But you knew she had money?'

'Well, I suspected it.'

'And not just her savings?'

'What do you mean? I don't understand.'

'Never mind. Did you ever try to borrow money from her?'

'Just once, I told you. When I was pregnant. And she gave me a hundred francs.'

'I'm thinking of more recently. You would have liked a little house in the country. Did you ever ask her to help you with that?'

'No. I can tell you didn't know her.'

'I've met her.'

'And like everyone else, you thought she was a charming old lady with a sweet smile and a timid air. Well, in reality, she was as tough as old boots.'

'Do you own a scarf with red stripes or checks on it?'

'No.'

'But there is, on the sofa in the living room, a cushion with red stripes, isn't there?'

'Maybe. Yes, I think so.'

'Why did you quarrel with your lover yesterday?'

'Because he was becoming impossible.'

'How do you mean?'

'When I meet a man for the first time, I don't ask him for a certificate of good behaviour. But Marcel went too far. He wasn't looking for work. He could have got himself a job behind a bar ten times over. He preferred to live with me and do nothing.'

'Did he know your aunt?'

'Needless to say, I never introduced him to her.'

'But he knew of her existence?'

'I suppose I must have mentioned her sometimes.'

'And said she would have some loot put by?'

' "Loot?" That's not the kind of thing I'd say!'

'Well, to sum it up: he did know where she lived and that there was a chance she'd have some savings at least.'

'Yes, probably.'

'Have you ever seen him on Quai de la Mégisserie?'

'No, never.'

'But he did go there. Two witnesses have reported seeing him.'

'In that case, you're better informed than me.'

'Was there ever any question of marriage between you?'

'Certainly not. Since I've had my son, I've never contemplated marrying. I take what I want from men, and it doesn't go any further. Do you understand what I'm saying?'

'Yes, I understand perfectly well. Now let's talk about the revolver.'

'What, again?'

'It's got to be somewhere, and I'm determined to find it. For a while, it was in the drawer of your aunt's bedside table. You claim that you didn't know that, and that your aunt was afraid of firearms.'

'That's right.'

'And yet she kept this weapon within reach, which by the way might suggest that she wasn't as indifferent to danger as you seem to think.'

'What are you getting at?'

Maigret began packing his pipe slowly.

'This morning, at your place, we found traces of this firearm, which must have been hidden for some time on top of your wardrobe.'

'That's what you say.'

'The forensic checks will establish it. Well, either you put it there, or your lover did.'

'I don't like that word.'

'It bothers you?'

'It's inaccurate There was no love between us.'

'Well, let's suppose that he did go to Quai de la Mégisserie.'

'To kill my aunt?'

'To find whatever it is that you don't like my calling her loot. The old lady gets back, finds herself face to face with an intruder. He uses a cushion from the couch to stifle her.'

'Well, why would he take the revolver? And hide it on my wardrobe? And then take it to Toulon with him?'

'You think he did?'

'If it really exists, it must, like you say, be somewhere. Now, I did *not* go to my aunt's house that afternoon she was killed. And I'm sure Marcel didn't either. He may not be as white as the driven snow, but he's not a killer. Have you got any more questions for me?'

'Have you sorted out the inheritance yet?'

'No. I'm due to go and see a lawyer this afternoon, who's the husband of one of my clients. I wouldn't have known how to find one otherwise.'

She stood up, looking relieved.

'When do I have to sign?'

'Your statement, you mean? How long, Lapointe?'

'It'll be typed up in half an hour.'

'Hear that? Go and sit in the waiting room.'

'Can't I come back to do that?'

'No, I want to get this over with. You'll have to be a bit late for the appointment with your lawyer, and by tonight you'll be richer by tens of thousands of francs. By the way, where are you going to live, in the apartment on Quai de la Mégisserie?'

'No, mine's all right for me.'

She moved towards the door, straight as a ramrod, and went out without another word.

He took the overnight train, and by good fortune found himself alone in his sleeper compartment. By the time they reached Montélimar, as the sun rose, he was awake, as always when he travelled to the south of France.

Montélimar was for him the border, where Provence began, and from then on he lost nothing of the landscape. He loved it all, the vegetation, the houses, pale pink or lavender blue, roofed with tiles that had been baked by the sun time and again, the villages with their plane trees, where already people were sitting in bars.

At Marseille, as the train manoeuvred into Gare Saint-Charles, he heard the sing-song accent of southerners, and everything seemed full of a special flavour to him.

It was a long time since he had brought his wife to the Côte d'Azur and he promised himself he would do that next time he had some leave. But alas, that would be in high summer, when everywhere would be crowded!

A few more kilometres and the sea appeared, as deep blue as on the postcards, with fishermen in their motionless boats.

Chief Inspector Marella was on the platform and waved energetically at him.

'Why don't you come down more often? How long is it since you've been to Toulon?'

'About ten years, like I said on the phone. I hope it doesn't bother you, that I'm here to make some inquiries on your patch?'

Maigret was outside his own jurisdiction. Here, Marella was the boss. His southern colleague was dark-haired, of course, not tall, but full of life. Since they had last met, he had acquired a small pot-belly, which made him look more bourgeois than in the past.

Back then, you might have been more likely to take him for a gangster than a policeman. Gangsters put on weight too, but by the time they reach that stage, they have generally retired from business.

'Would you like a coffee?'

'Good idea. I had some in the train but it was awful.'

'Let's go across the square, then.'

The square was already dazzling in the warm sunlight. They went into a café and sat at the counter.

'So what have you got to tell me?'

'Nothing. It's a strange case, and I seem to be wading through mud. Where's Marcel right now?'

'In bed. He was celebrating half the night with friends at the Victor Restaurant. across the way from the Port-Marchand. Petty crooks, the lot of them. Around midnight, some girls joined them.'

'Did you know him when he lived here?'

'He never stayed very long in Toulon. Two years was the most he spent here. I should say that the local gangs don't take him too seriously. They think he's an amateur.'

'So who is this Bob who acts as a letterbox?'

'The barman at the Amiral. He keeps his nose pretty clean, I think. At any rate, neither I nor my men have ever been able to pin anything on him.'

'And the Giovanni brothers?'

'Just one of them is still here, the older one, Pepito. The other, so I've been told, lives in the Paris region now. Pepito bought a luxury villa from an elderly American woman who wanted to go home to die. It's the grandest villa in Sanary, with a private harbour where he moors his yacht.

'He sees very few people, and almost never his old associates. He wants us to forget all about him. Still, I keep an eye on him. As he well knows, and if we meet in the street, he always greets me warmly.'

'I wonder what Marcel went to see him about.'

'Me too, I'd really like to know. Especially since Marcel has never worked with him in the past.'

'Remind me which hotel he's staying in.'

'Hôtel des Cinq Continents, Avenue de la République, very near the Préfecture Maritime.'

It was only eight in the morning.

'Do you want to come with me to pay him a visit? That'll give you some idea of what this case is about. He'll be furious at being woken up so early.'

Maigret had not booked an overnight stay, since he planned to return to Paris that same evening. Marella obtained the number of Marcel's room, and they went up together and knocked loudly at the door. It was some time before a sleepy voice asked:

'What's the matter?'

'Police!'

Marella had replied, and Marcel, barefoot and in rumpled pyjamas, dragged himself over to the door and opened it.

'Well, well, look who's here,' he muttered, eyeing Maigret. 'But since Inspector Marella is with you . . .'

He went over to open the curtains, lit a cigarette and moved a pair of trousers from one of the armchairs.

'So what have I done now?' he asked.

'Nothing new, probably.'

'By the way,' Marella intervened, speaking to Marcel, 'yesterday afternoon, you went to visit the gorgeous Maria. So you didn't know that she's been hanging out with La Grêle for the last few weeks?'

'Yeah, and he's in jail.'

'I arrested him last week, yes, and this time it's serious, drug trafficking. But he has friends outside. And you're not from these parts.'

'Thanks for the tip. I've known Maria for years. What about you, Monsieur Maigret? Why have you come all this way, when we met only the day before yesterday?'

'Possibly to escort you back to Paris.'

'What? Are you joking?'

'There's the matter of the key, first of all.'

'What key?'

'The key to the old lady's apartment. Who was it that took the impression of the lock? That's not something Angèle would have been up to doing.'

Marcel did not move a muscle.

'Very well. You'll have to make a statement with a stenographer and sign it.'

'For Christ's sake, I've got nothing to do with this whole damn business! OK, I was living with the gendarme. Waiting for something better to turn up, I've made no secret of that, and I'm darned glad to be rid of her.'

'At least two witnesses have recognized you.'

'How could they recognize me?'

'From a photo of you we have on file, or rather the Vice Squad does.'

'And who might these two witnesses be?'

'The bird-seller downstairs, and the tenant from the same landing as the old lady. She says you bumped into her rushing upstairs without looking, and you apologized.'

'Well, they must have been seeing things, the pair of them.'

'You were wearing the checked suit you had on yesterday.'

'You can find suits like that in any big store. There must be I don't know how many in Paris alone.'

'So you didn't have a key? Did you pick the lock?'

'Is this going to take long?'

'I don't know. Why?'

'Because if it is, I'll get them to bring up some coffee and croissants.'

He called room service and placed his order.

'And don't expect me to offer you anything. I haven't picked any lock, and I wouldn't even know how to do it.'

'When did she tell you about the revolver?'

'Who?'

'You know perfectly well who. Angèle. You wouldn't have guessed on your own that there'd be a revolver in the old woman's place.'

'I had no idea she even existed.'

'Wrong. Angèle herself admitted it, in her signed statement, and she told us she pointed out her aunt's windows to you, and said she was due to inherit from her one day.'

'And you believed her? You don't know that that woman's a born liar.'

'What about you?'

'I'm telling you the truth. I can't afford to take a false step, because the police are always sniffing round me. And what proves it is this photo you found at the Vice Squad, that I don't even remember.'

The waiter brought in coffee and croissants and a fragrant

smell filled the room. Sitting at a small table, still barefoot and in pyjamas, Marcel started eating his breakfast.

Marella glanced at Maigret, as if asking permission to say something.

'What were you talking to Bob about?'

'When I got here last night, we chatted about this and that, catching up on our news. We're old mates and we haven't seen each other for ages.'

'And what else?'

'I don't know what you mean.'

'Which of the two of you brought up Giovanni's name?'

'Could have been me. Used to know him back in the old days, when I was a kid and he lived in Montmartre.'

'So in that case, why wasn't it you that phoned him?'

'Why would I phone him?'

'To make an appointment with him. Bob did it for you. What story did you give him?'

'I've no idea what you're talking about.'

'Don't play the idiot. You know perfectly well you don't just roll up at Giovanni's door, especially if you're just a small-time crook, short of money. And yet yesterday, you went to see him and stayed most of an hour.'

'We were just chatting.'

'And what were you chatting about?'

The small-time crook was getting nervous. He didn't like the direction the questions were taking.

'Look, it was like this, I was asking if he had any jobs for me. He's got a lot of businesses, all on the level, I should say. He might have been needing someone he could trust.'

'And he hired you?'

'He said he'd think about it, and let me know in a day or two.'

Marella looked at Maigret again, to indicate that he had finished.

'You heard what my colleague Chief Inspector Marella said just now. He will give instructions to his colleagues. You'll go down to the station and repeat all you've just told us. You'll wait for your statement to be typed up and then sign it. Try not to leave anything out, especially concerning Bob and Giovanni.'

'Do I have to mention his name?'

'Why, were you lying?'

'No, no. But he won't like it if I've mentioned his name to the police.'

'You've no choice about that. And don't you leave Toulon until we give you permission.'

'Oh, all very well for you! If I can't find any work, will you pay my hotel bills?'

'We might offer you board and lodging in a different kind of hotel,' Marella intervened. 'You'd be very comfortable there, plenty of shade from the sun.'

The two policemen returned to the street.

'I hope I wasn't interfering too much with things that aren't my business,' said Marella, a little anxiously.

'Not at all. On the contrary, you did me a good turn. You can do the same with Bob.'

They hadn't far to go, just across the Avenue de la République. The Amiral was at the corner of the sea front and a narrow street inaccessible to cars. Outside on the pavement were four café tables, covered in checked cloths.

By contrast with the sunshine outside, made more dazzling by the light reflecting off the sea, the interior seemed dark and it was agreeably cool.

A barman with a boxer's broken nose and cauliflower ears was rinsing glasses. At this time of day, there was not a single customer, and a waiter was laying the tables.

'Good morning, inspector. What can I get you?'

He was addressing Marella, since he didn't know Maigret.

'Do you have some Provençal wine?' Maigret asked him.

'Rosé? By the carafe.'

'Two rosés. Or a carafe. As you like.'

They were both quite relaxed and Bob was the only one not feeling at ease.

'Now then, Bob, you had a visitor, evening before last.'

'Oh, here, you know, we're never short of visitors.'

'I don't mean a customer. I mean someone who came down from Paris especially to see you.'

'To see me?'

'Well, to ask you for a favour.'

'I don't see what kind of favour I could do him.'

'Have you known him long?'

'Seven or eight years.'

'And his nose is clean?'

'He's never been in prison. His record's clean as a whistle.'

'And yours?'

'Not entirely, as you well know.'

'And what did he want?'

'He was just passing through and he called in for a chat.'

'He asked you to make a phone call.'

'Ah!'

'Don't play the innocent, Bob. One of my men was in here, and watched you go to the cabin while your pal waited. And it was a long call. He looked nervous. When you came back and whispered something to him, he seemed relieved.'

'That'll have been about an old flame of his, Maria. He went to see her.'

'And she lives in Sanary, does she?'

'No, of course not.'

'It's not in your interest to clam up on us, Bob. You phoned Pepito Giovanni, a man you used to work for, before he hung up his fancy loafers. And you got an interview with him for your pal Marcel. Which was quite something, because Giovanni doesn't agree to meet just anyone, especially on his home ground. So what did you tell him?'

'Giovanni? Just that I had someone here who was looking for work.'

'No!'

'Why do you say no?'

'Because you know quite well that's not true. And Giovanni will be the first to laugh when I tell him.'

'I said my friend had a deal to offer him. Absolutely above board.'

'And you saw the sample?'

'No.'

'But you know what it was about?'

'Marcel didn't say. He just told me it was a very, very big deal. International. Could interest people in America.'

'That's better, perhaps I'm beginning to believe you now. And Giovanni was interested, was he?'

'He said to send my friend up to see him yesterday at three.'

'And that's all?'

'He said to tell him not to forget to bring the goods, and to be sure to come on his own.'

The rosé wine was cool and fruity. Maigret listened to the conversation, a vague smile on his lips. He'd always liked Marella, who, if he had stayed in Paris, might be sitting at his own desk in Quai des Orfèvres. But the southerner was really in his element in Toulon. He'd been born in Nice. He knew all the criminals and prostitutes between Menton and Marseille.

'Anything else you want to ask him, Maigret?'

Bob frowned.

'You mean this is Detective Chief Inspector Maigret?'

'Precisely. And he's the one you'll have to deal with if you're not lucky.'

'My apologies for not recognizing you.'

And as Maigret was getting out his wallet:

'No, no, this is on the house.'

'Out of the question!'

He put a ten-franc note on the table.

'And I expect the minute we're out of here you'll be on the phone to Giovanni?'

'Not if you ask me not to. I wouldn't want to get into any trouble with him. And not with Chief Inspector Marella either.'

They were soon back outside in the sunshine, among sailors with blue collars and red pompoms.

'You'd like us to visit Giovanni now? Sure you wouldn't prefer to go on your own?'

'No, on the contrary.'

'In that case, let's go by way of the station and get my car.'

They crossed the Seyne, where a ship was being broken up, and found themselves looking across at the Sanary peninsula, where a large villa was visible at the far end.

'That's where he lives. If Bob hasn't phoned him, Marcel will have. And he'll be a tougher nut to crack.'

6.

He came towards them through the immense sun-filled lounge. He was wearing a cream silk suit and approached with his hand outstretched.

'Good day to you, Marella,' he said to the local police chief.

Then, pretending not to have noticed Maigret before:

'Well, well! Monsieur Maigret. I wasn't expecting the honour of a visit from you.'

He was a good-looking man, strongly built but carrying no extra fat. He must have been about sixty, but, at first sight, one could take him for fifty.

The room had been tastefully furnished, no doubt by an interior decorator, and its proportions made it look rather like a stage set.

'Where would you like to sit? In here or on the terrace?'

He led them out to the terrace, where some luxurious reclining chairs were shaded by parasols.

A butler in a white jacket had followed them and stood waiting, almost to attention.

'Let me offer you something. What would you say to a Tom Collins? At this time of day, that's still the most refreshing drink.'

Maigret indicated that he would accept one and Marella followed suit.

'Two Tom Collinses, Georges, and the usual for me.'

He was close-shaven and his hands were well cared for, the nails impeccably manicured.

'You arrived this morning?' he asked Maigret as if engaging in casual conversation. He seemed quite relaxed.

They could see the sea stretching out to infinity and a motor yacht rocking gently in the little private harbour beneath them.

'I came on the overnight train.'

'Don't tell me that it was just to see me.'

'I didn't know when I arrived in Toulon that I'd be paying you a visit.'

'I'm all the more flattered.'

Despite his friendly manner, one could sense in his eyes a certain steeliness which he was doing his best to conceal under a veneer of cordiality.

'So you're away from your usual stamping ground, inspector?'

'Very true. But my friend Marella here is on his own territory.'

'And we get on extremely well, Marella and I. Don't we, Marella?'

'As long as you give me no cause to trouble you.'

'I lead such a quiet life! As you know, I hardly ever go out. This house has almost become my entire world. A friend might call now and then, a pretty girl on occasion.'

'And would you count Marcel, known as Big Marcel, as one of your friends?'

He assumed a shocked air.

'That shabby character who came to see me yesterday?'

'But you did allow him to visit.'

'Because, on principle, I prefer to give everyone a chance in life. In days gone by, I've needed a helping hand myself.'

'And that's what you gave him?'

The butler returned with two large frosted tumblers and a smaller glass containing tomato juice.

'You will have to excuse me, I never touch alcohol. Your very good health. I believe you had just asked me a question.'

'I asked you whether you gave a helping hand to your visitor.'

'Unfortunately, no. I can't see a job for him in any of my businesses. You see, Monsieur Maigret, these days I've become a businessman, and a lot of water has flowed under the Pont-Neuf since we last met.

'I own twelve cinemas on the Côte d'Azur, including two in Marseille, one in Nice, one in Antibes and three in Cannes, not to mention the one in Aix-en-Provence. And I have a nightclub in Marseille, plus three hotels, one of them in Menton. All of them perfectly in order with the authorities, is that not so, Marella?'

'Perfectly.'

'And I have a restaurant in Paris, Avenue de la Grande-Armée, near the Arc de Triomphe, which my brother runs. It's a very elegant restaurant with excellent fare, and you are cordially invited there whenever you wish.'

Maigret was looking at him imperturbably.

'As you might imagine, I wouldn't have a job in any of those concerns for a third-rate little pimp.'

'Did he leave the sample with you?'

Giovanni, despite his self-control, could not help registering this with a slight movement.

'What sample do you mean? Perhaps this is a case of mistaken identity?'

'You arranged for Marcel to come and see you, because Bob the barman phoned you and informed you about some very big deal, something of international proportions.'

'I'm afraid I don't understand. Was it Bob who told you this fantastic story?'

'It was something that might interest the Americans.'

'But I don't do any business with Americans.'

'I'm going to tell you a little tale, Giovanni, and I hope you will derive some profit from it. There was once upon a time in Paris a charming old lady, who got it into her head that certain objects in her apartment had been moved when she was out.'

'I don't see where—'

'Wait. The old lady came and asked police headquarters for protection, and at first we thought she was a little mad. Still, I did intend to call round, if only to reassure her.'

'Ah, I might have read about something like this in the papers.'

'Yes, it was mentioned but just in a small paragraph, and they didn't know the details.'

'A cigar?'

'Thank you, but I prefer my pipe.'

'Marella, what about you?'

'Gladly, thank you.'

There was a box of Havanas on the table and the two men each took a cigar.

'Forgive me, I didn't mean to interrupt you. So, you went to see this old lady.'

'No, I haven't got there yet.'

'I'm listening.'

'She had a niece, a middle-aged woman with a pronounced taste for younger men. For almost six months now, for instance, she's been living with this man, Marcel, whom you received here yesterday.'

Giovanni started to look interested.

'Well, the old lady was murdered before I had had the chance to make my promised visit.'

'What kind of murder?'

'She was smothered. Someone pressed a cushion against her face. At her age, she wasn't able to resist for long.'

'I'm wondering what any of this has to do with me.'

'I told you that Marcel was the niece's lover. Two witnesses have stated that they saw him, at least once, inside the building where the aunt lived.'

'Do you suspect him of having killed her?'

'Either him or the niece. It comes to more or less the same thing.'

'What were they after, then?'

'The sample.'

'And that is . . . ?'

'The object that Marcel showed you.'

'What kind of object?'

'You know better than I do, since there's a strong chance it's in your possession at this time.'

'I still don't understand.'

'The object is a revolver. I will admit right away that I don't know any of its details, or what makes it so significant.'

'I've never owned a gun in my life, as you should know. In the old days when I was a young tearaway, I was often questioned by the police, and no one has ever been able to charge me with carrying an unlicensed gun.'

'Yes. I know that.'

'So in that case, I fail to see why I would have accepted a revolver offered me by some lowlife.'

'Don't worry. I'm not going to ask my friend Marella to have your villa searched from cellar to attic. You are far too prudent to have left this object somewhere where we might discover it.'

'Thanks for the compliment. Another Tom Collins?'

'One's enough, thank you.'

Marella had never seen Maigret work in such a low-key way. He was speaking in a quietly casual voice, as if he attached no importance to his words, yet you could tell that every one of them counted.

'I wasn't expecting, when I came here today, that you would admit the purpose of Marcel's visit. I simply intended to warn you. He can't have told you that this revolver is closely connected to a murder. An unpremeditated one, actually. The old lady, who used to go and sit on a bench in the Tuileries Gardens in the afternoon, returned home sooner than usual, for some reason. She surprised the visitor, man or woman—'

'You mean it could be the niece?'

'That's right, the niece. Whoever it was grabbed a cushion and pressed it down on the old lady's face for as long as it took. So you see now how this "international" affair would not look well alongside your present activities, I mean your cinemas, hotels, restaurants and so on.'

Maigret stopped speaking and looked at him calmly. Giovanni was rather unsettled but managed not to let it show too much.

'I must thank you for the warning. If that fellow comes back here, he'll immediately be shown the door.'

'He won't come back unless you send him a message, and I know that you won't do such a thing.'

'Did you know about this, Marella?'

'I found out about it yesterday.'

'And you've told your colleague Maigret that I have become an important businessman, in good standing with all the regional authorities, including the prefect?'

'Yes. I told him.'

'It only remains for me to repeat that this affair has nothing to do with me.'

Maigret stood up with a sigh.

'Thanks for the Tom Collins.'

Marella rose in turn and Giovanni walked them through the large lounge to the marble staircase outside.

'You will always be welcome, gentlemen.'

They got back into the car.

'Don't go too far,' Maigret said to Marella, as they drove out of the grounds. 'There must be some café somewhere where we would have a view of the villa's harbour.'

They did not leave Sanary but stopped in front of a

blue-fronted bistro outside which four men were playing pétanque.

'What'll you have?'

'A glass of rosé. The Tom Collins left me with a nasty taste in the mouth.'

'I didn't understand what you were doing,' Marella said quietly. 'You didn't press him. You looked as if you were believing what he said.'

'In the first place, he's not the kind of man who would talk.'

'True.'

'And what have I got against him? He agreed to see this petty crook after a phone call from Bob the barman. I don't even know what the revolver looks like.'

'Does it really exist?'

'It exists all right. It was when they were looking for it that the old lady's visitors moved things around in her apartment. But can you see us, even with all your men, turning up at that big barn of a villa with a search warrant? Would Giovanni just have put it in a drawer in his bedside table? We'll soon see if I'm right.'

They did see, a quarter of an hour later. A man in a peaked sailor's cap went down to the little yacht and the engine started almost at once.

A few moments later, Giovanni was making his way down the harbour steps and going aboard.

'It's too hot for him to handle, do you see? He's in a hurry to get rid of it. Anyway, the deal's a nonstarter now.'

The yacht left the harbour and set out to sea, cutting a powerful swathe through the water.

'In a few minutes' time, the revolver will be at the bottom of the Mediterranean, God knows how many metres down. No chance of finding it.'

'I see.'

'So, really, now I'm finished with the Toulon end of the case.'

'I hope you'll have dinner with us. We have a spare bedroom these days, unlike when you were last here.'

'I'm taking the night train back.'

'Do you have to?'

'Pretty much. I'll have a busy day tomorrow.'

'The niece?'

'Among other things. Can you keep Marcel in your sights? And it wouldn't be a bad idea to keep an eye on your man Bob, who seems to me to have a lot more going on than minding the bar. Do you think Giovanni's affairs are really above board?'

'I've been trying to nab him for years. Characters like that, even when they start acting like choirboys, always keep in discreet touch with the underworld. As you just saw.'

The white yacht, having traced a wide circle out at sea, was already returning to harbour.

'He must be feeling better now he's got rid of the famous "sample".'

'What are you planning to do before you catch your train?'

'I'd like to see Marcel again. Do you think he's likely to be at Maria's place?'

'No, that'd surprise me. After what he was told about

her current boyfriend, he'll be wary. He's a false tough guy – he doesn't actually like to take risks.'

'The Amiral, then?'

'He might well go there, yes.'

By the time they reached the bar it was five in the afternoon, another quiet time for business. Bob wasn't behind the bar, but sitting at a table opposite Marcel.

The latter could not suppress an exclamation on seeing the two policemen.

'What, again!'

'Yes indeed, again. We'll have a carafe of rosé, Bob.'

'How many times do I have to tell you I didn't kill the old bird?'

'Happy to take your word for it, sunshine. Doesn't alter the fact that we've got you placed at Quai de la Mégisserie.'

Maigret had chosen to address him familiarly, in a jocular tone.

'I'm still waiting for you to offer any proof of that. And for you to tell me what I'm supposed to have been doing there.'

'The sample.'

'I don't get it.'

'Someone a lot smarter than you, just now, didn't get it either. And yet he's been around a long time.'

'You went to see Giovanni?'

Marcel had turned pale. Bob was returning to the table with glasses and a carafe.

'What did he say?'

'Something about an international affair, was it? One that might interest the Americans in particular?'

'I don't know what you're talking about.'

'Never mind. But I should warn you that there's no point now your going along to the villa in Sanary, hoping to get a sum of money of any kind.'

'You saw Giovanni?' Bob asked in turn as he sat down.

'Just come away from there.'

'And he was willing to tell you he'd seen Marcel?'

'And that you had telephoned him.'

Maigret was drinking the rosé de Provence in small sips. Another two hours and the train would be taking him back to Paris.

He turned to Marcel again.

'If you really didn't kill the old lady, I strongly advise you to tell the whole truth and to come back to Paris with me.'

The man's long hands were clenched nervously.

'What do you think, Bob?'

'It's nothing to do with me. I was just helping out a friend, that's all. I don't know anything about this business.'

'Why should I come back to Paris?' Marcel asked.

'For a stay in the cells.'

'But I already told you—'

'I know, I know. It wasn't you that killed the old lady. But if it was her niece, then you can still be charged with aiding and abetting.'

'And you're advising me to leave Toulon, so as to be arrested?'

'It's possible that staying here might be a less safe bet.'

The man looked cocky.

'No, inspector. I'm not that stupid. If you've got an

arrest warrant, show me, and you can take me away. You know very well you can't do that, because you've got no evidence, apart from these two so-called witnesses who saw a checked suit on the stairs.'

'As you wish.'

'That's what I get for keeping my nose clean for years.'

'You'd have done better to go on keeping it clean.'

This time Marella paid for the drinks. Then he looked at his watch.

'There's still time for you to come and say hello to my wife. And you can see our new house.'

It was out of town on a hill. The villa wasn't large but it was very attractive and welcoming.

A boy of about fifteen was mowing the lawn and his machine made a noise like a huge insect.

'You know my son, Alain.'

'He was a baby when I saw him last.'

'As you can see, the baby's grown up.'

They went inside to the large living room. Madame Marella came out of her kitchen, a rolling pin in her hand.

'Oh, sorry! I didn't know you'd brought a guest.'

Maigret kissed her on both cheeks. Her name was Claudine, and he had never seen her without a smile on her lips.

'You'll stay for dinner, I hope? I'm just making a strawberry tart.'

'No, he's catching the overnight train back to Paris.'

'Have you been down here long, Monsieur Maigret?'

'Just since this morning.'

'And you're going back already?'

'Thanks to your husband, who has been a great help to me.'

'What can we offer you?' said Marella. 'I notice you didn't turn your nose up at our Provençal wine. I've got some in the cellar that's a lot better than what you get at the Amiral.'

The two men spent an hour together chatting about this and that. Fifteen-year-old Alain came to shake Maigret's hand.

'Not in school?'

'Perhaps you've forgotten that it's Saturday?'

And it was true, Maigret had forgotten. The events of the week had been linked in such a way that he hadn't kept track of the days.

'What class are you in now?'

'Fourth year, Latin stream.'

'Do you want to follow your father into the police force?'

'Oh no! We never know what time he's going to come home, and when you've gone to bed, there's always a risk the phone will ring and wake you up.'

Maigret felt melancholy. He would have liked to have a son too, even if the son didn't want to join the police.

'I'd better be going. I don't want to miss my train.'

'I'll give you a lift to the station.'

A few moments later, they were driving away from the villa, leaving Claudine waving goodbye from the steps.

When the taxi stopped on Boulevard Richard-Lenoir, virtually deserted on a Sunday morning, the sound of the car door slamming was enough to make Madame Maigret hasten to the open window.

She was waiting for him on the landing.

'I thought you'd be spending the night in Toulon. Why didn't you phone to say you'd be back?'

'I wanted to give you a surprise.'

With a scarf round her hair, she was doing the housework.

'Not too tired?'

'Not at all, I slept very well.'

'Would you like me to run you a bath?'

'Yes, please.'

He had shaved on the train, as he always did, before getting to Paris.

'Did you get the result you were after?'

'More or less. By the way, Marella and Claudine send you their kind regards. They've had a little villa built, very nice, just out of town.'

'Is Claudine as cheerful as ever?'

'She hasn't changed at all. Only the son has, he's a teenager now with a deep voice.'

'Are you free all day today?'

'Almost. But I'll have to go out for a while later.'

While the bath was filling, he called the Police Judiciaire, and once more it was the dependable Lucas on duty.

'Nothing to report your end?'

'Nothing special, chief.'

'Who've you got there at the moment?'

'Neveu, Janin, Lourtie . . .'

'No need to go on, I don't need that many. I want them to make sure between them that there's someone day and night to keep an eye on the building where Angèle Louette, the masseuse, lives. Rue Saint-André-des-Arts. No need to hide. But don't forget she has a car.'

He stayed a long while under the bubbles of the bath water, while his wife made coffee. At about half past nine, he went downstairs and took a taxi, stopping at one end of Rue Saint-André-des-Arts. Janin was the man on duty and he went over to shake hands.

'I'm going up to see her, and it's possible that what I say to her might make her want to disappear.'

'Don't worry, chief, I'll keep my eyes open. Neveu and I have agreed what to do. Rather than have long stints, we'll relieve each other every three hours, and tonight Lourtie will come and lend a hand.'

Maigret went upstairs and rang the bell: the door opened almost immediately.

Angèle Louette was wearing her dark suit and putting on a hat.

'What, you again!' she groaned. 'Can't you leave me alone for a single day?'

'Were you just going out?'

'Yes, as you can see. I don't wear a hat to do the house-work.'

'I'm just back from Toulon.'

'What's that got to do with me?'

'You should be very interested, as a matter of fact. Your lover had driven himself down there, and we met up.'

'We won't be having any more to do with each other.'

144

'Yes, you will. Since he was the one who was going to handle negotiations with Giovanni.'

She couldn't help giving a little jump.

'Negotiations that failed, let me say straight away, so your aunt was killed for nothing. Do you know where the revolver is now? At the bottom of the Mediterranean, dozens or hundreds of metres down. Did Marcel not telephone to tell you?'

'If he'd phoned me to say you were on your way, you wouldn't have found me in.'

'Where are you going now?'

'To Mass, if you must know. And too bad if that surprises you.'

'I have a message for you. You're to present yourself at my office at nine tomorrow morning. I advise you not to be late. And I'd also suggest you bring an overnight bag, because it's possible we'll be holding you for a while.'

'Do you mean that you're going to arrest me?'

'That's one possible outcome. Which doesn't depend on me, but on the examining magistrate. One more thing, then I'll let you go. There's been a police watch on you for the last hour and that will continue until you come to my office tomorrow morning.'

'I hate you.'

'I'd expect nothing less from you.'

As Maigret went downstairs, he could hear her pacing round her living room, talking vehemently to herself.

'Do you know what she looks like?' he asked Janin.

'No.'

'I'll wait here to show you, because she'll be down shortly.'

She stayed another ten minutes in her apartment. When she emerged and saw the two men standing opposite she gave a violent start.

'Easy to recognize, as you see. If she was a boxer, she'd be a heavyweight.'

He returned home on foot in the sunlit peacefulness of Sunday morning. He wondered what they would do that afternoon. They sometimes went out in the car, with Madame Maigret driving, but she was nervous of taking the wheel on Sunday, especially outside the city.

Well, it didn't matter what they did. Even if it was just a walk side by side along the streets, they were never bored.

'You missed him by five minutes. Your friend Marella rang up. He wants you to call him back as soon as possible, on his home number. Apparently he gave it to you.'

She looked hard at her husband.

'Doesn't it strike you as odd that he's phoned on a Sunday morning when you only saw him last night?'

'I was rather expecting it.'

He asked for a line to Toulon and a few minutes later was speaking to Marella.

'How was your journey?'

'After your rosé de Provence, I slept like a baby.'

'I expect you can guess why I've called.'

'What happened to him?'

'He was pulled out of the harbour at seven this morning.'

'Stabbed?'

'No. A .38 bullet in the forehead.'

There was a silence, as both men digested their own thoughts.

'You were doing him a real favour by advising him to come to Paris with you. But he thought he was being clever. That you were lying, and he could still get something out of the deal.'

'I suppose Giovanni is untouchable?'

'He'll have taken precautions, as you've no doubt worked out. In fact, I'm ready to swear the hired gun won't even know who he was working for. The instructions must have gone through a third party.'

'Any idea who it was?'

'Plenty of choice. There are about twenty characters on the Côte d'Azur who could have taken on the job. Someone was probably brought in from Nice, Cannes or Marseille. And whoever it was won't be in Toulon by now. He managed not to be seen.'

Marella paused reflectively.

'Well, we'll get him sooner or later, but it could be in four or five years, for something quite different.'

'Same here, of course. Thanks for giving me the news. Were you there when they emptied his pockets?'

'Yes, nothing special. Two thousand francs in the wallet, with his driving licence and ID. The motor insurance was in the glove compartment of the car, which was parked all night outside the Hôtel des Cinq Continents. Some small change. A key.'

'I'd like you to send me the key.'

'It'll go off straight away. I'll post it from the station. Apart from that, a handkerchief, cigarettes, chewing gum.'

'Did you open his suitcase?'

'Spare suit, black and white checks, underwear. No papers. Just a cheap novel in a jazzy cover.'

'No address book with phone numbers?'

'No. But it's possible I wasn't the first on the scene. According to the doc, he was killed at about one a.m. That's just a guess. He'll be doing the post-mortem this afternoon.'

'Claudine's not too cross with me, is she?'

'Why would she be?'

'Because of me, your Sunday morning has been spoilt.'

'She's in the kitchen. Ah, she's telling me to say hello to you and your wife. Well, the case is off my hands now. I'll let my deputy carry out the routine investigation.'

'Have you seen Bob again?'

'No. I'm hoping he's not met the same fate. That would be unfortunate, because he's been regular, as far as we're concerned.'

'I think he's too valuable to Giovanni.'

'You're thinking what I'm thinking? There must be someone who's the link between Giovanni and the criminal networks.'

'Bob's well placed for that, isn't he?'

'Well, goodbye, then.'

'Goodbye. And thanks very much for all your help.'

Maigret hung up.

'Bad news?' asked Madame Maigret, seeing her husband looking preoccupied.

'Well, professionally I ought to say it's excellent news. A man has been shot dead in Toulon, and his death means we don't have to drag him to court. An ex-pimp who was living off a woman of fifty-five. If he didn't commit the murder himself, he must have been an accomplice in it at the very least.'

'The old lady's murder, you mean?'

Yes, he thought, the old lady with the white hat and gloves. He could picture her again on Quai des Orfèvres, suddenly appearing alongside him on the pavement, her eyes shining with admiration and hope.

She was dead. And now Marcel, known as Big Marcel, was dead too, and the object the couple had been searching for, the famous revolver, which had just been lying in a bedside drawer, was lost for good.

'What's for lunch?'

'Blanquette of veal.'

They passed the time until half past twelve. Maigret even switched on the radio, but of course the dead man in Toulon was not mentioned.

'Do you want to go to the cinema?' she asked.

'Don't you think it's too fine an afternoon to spend it sitting indoors?'

'What would you like to do, then?'

'Let's go out and then we'll see.'

She took his arm as usual and they walked down towards the river. This meant going past Quai de la Mégisserie, where the bird-seller's shop was shuttered up.

'Which floor was it on?'

'First.'

'That'll make someone happy.'

'What do you mean?'

'Whoever gets to rent that apartment. They'll have one of the best views in Paris from their windows.'

They carried on walking and before long arrived at the Tuileries Gardens.

'Shall we sit down for a few minutes?' he suggested.

And thus he was able to fulfil a wish he had entertained since the previous evening. He couldn't remember ever sitting down on a public bench. Indeed, he would not have been far off thinking that benches were of little use, except for tramps to sleep on, or lovers to meet.

They took quite some time to find one that was free. All the others were occupied, and not only by old people. There were many young mothers with their children. On one bench, a man of about thirty was reading a biology textbook.

'It's nice here, isn't it?'

Toy yachts with white sails were criss-crossing the clear water of the pond.

'Hubert, don't get wet! If you lean over like that you'll fall in!'

Relaxing, wasn't it? Seen from here, life seemed simple and uncomplicated.

The old lady had come here every day, weather permitting. Like another old lady sitting opposite them, she probably threw down breadcrumbs for the birds, which were coming closer and closer.

'It's because of her that you wanted to come here?'

'Yes,' he admitted. 'And also I wanted for once in my life to sit down on a bench.'

He added quickly:

'Especially with you.'

'You've got a short memory.'

'Why, have we done this before?'

'When we were engaged, we sat down on a bench in Place des Vosges. Actually, that was the first time you kissed me.'

'You're right. And I have got a short memory. I'd kiss you again, but there are too many people about.'

'And it's not quite the proper thing at our age, is it?'

They did not go home for dinner. Instead they ate at a little restaurant, a favourite of theirs, on Place des Victoires.

'Shall we stay out on the terrace?'

'I wouldn't advise it,' the waiter intervened. 'It gets cold quite quickly in the evening. It's not a good idea to dine outside just yet.'

They enjoyed their sweetbreads, which were delicious, followed by some tiny lamb chops and, to finish, a strawberry dessert.

'This doesn't often happen,' Madame Maigret murmured.

'What doesn't?'

'That you have almost all day to spend with me. I'm sure tomorrow you'll be phoning to say you won't be back for lunch.'

'That's possible. Or even probable. I'm going to have to confront the "gendarme".'

'Is that what you call the poor woman?'

'A poor woman who probably killed her aunt.'

'But it wasn't premeditated, was it?'

'No.'

'She must have panicked when she was discovered.'

'Are you going to defend her?'

'No, but I've thought about her a few times. You said she was very plain.'

'Well, let's say she's charmless.'

'And she was like that when she was young too?'

'Yes, certainly.'

'Because men didn't come courting her, she had to resign herself to taking another approach with them.'

'You'd make a good lawyer.'

'Fifty-five, you said? She probably thought this Marcel was her last chance, and she clung to him with all her might.'

'Well, she's still clinging, because she doesn't yet know what's happened to him.'

'You don't think she'll try to run away?'

'I've got an inspector stationed outside her door.'

'I wouldn't like to be in your shoes tomorrow.'

'I'd rather be somewhere else too.'

It was his job, and Angèle Louette was not the kind of woman who inspires pity.

Madame Maigret understood her husband's train of thought when he murmured:

'By the way, Marella's son is determined not to go into the police.'

What would he have advised his own son, if he had one?

They walked back arm in arm to Boulevard Richard-Lenoir, and for a long time neither of them spoke.

7.

When, at exactly nine in the morning, old Joseph ushered her into his office, Maigret looked at her differently from the previous times, feeling a little awkward, perhaps because he was remembering his wife's words from the evening before.

He even stood up to greet her, and the small suitcase she was holding gave her an almost pathetic air.

She looked pale, but then she always did. And yes, plain. Would he have been so hard on her if she had been a pretty woman?

'Put down your case, and take a seat.'

Everything was ready and Lapointe at the other end of the desk was prepared to take shorthand notes of the interrogation.

'It's nine o'clock now, isn't it? I've already had to cancel an eight o'clock client. And I have another due at nine. You're taking away my livelihood.'

The previous day, as he knew from his inspectors, she had gone straight home from Mass, and had not left the building again. The light had been on in her apartment until quite late into the night.

No one had visited. She had spent all those hours waiting on her own.

Was that why she now looked more serious and somehow overwhelmed?

He picked up the telephone.

'Can you see if Examining Magistrate Libart has arrived?'

He heard the phone ringing unanswered.

'Not yet, sir. His clerk isn't there either.'

'Thank you.'

He lit his pipe and said to Angèle Louette:

'You're free to smoke if you wish to.'

'How kind of you. The condemned man's cigarette, I suppose.'

'Mademoiselle, it's time for us to get to the bottom of this case. I may be asking you questions I've put to you before, but it will, I hope, be for the last time.'

It was as if even the weather had conspired to make this confrontation grey and gloomy in atmosphere. Whereas the previous two weeks had been radiant, today the sky was dark and a fine rain was falling over Paris.

'I presume you agree that your aunt was murdered?'

'I can't argue with the conclusions of the police pathologist.'

'Do you know of any enemies she might have had?'

'No.'

She was calm, sullenly calm, like the weather. Her face was expressionless and she was looking steadfastly at Maigret, hiding her emotions, that is, if she felt any.

It was as though her long lonely wait on Sunday had drained all her combative spirit.

'Friends?'

'I didn't know of any friends either.'

'Were you the only person to whom she opened the door of her apartment on Quai de la Mégisserie?'

'To my knowledge, yes.'

'You didn't let her know in advance when you were going to visit?'

'My aunt didn't have a phone. I wanted her to put one in, but she always refused.'

'Why did you go to see her?'

'I was her only relative.'

She was still wearing her black suit, which made her look as though she was in mourning.

'And you knew when you might find her at home?'

'Yes.'

'You were familiar with her timetable?'

'It was always the same.'

'In the morning, she went shopping locally, didn't she?'

'That's right.'

'And after lunch, if I remember correctly, she would take a nap in her armchair.'

She nodded.

'Then, if the weather was fine, she would go to the Tuileries Gardens and sit on a bench.'

'We've already been through all this, haven't we?'

'I have my reasons for going through it again. And you were not fond of her?'

'No.'

'You still resented the measly hundred francs she gave you long ago when you asked her for help because you were expecting a child?'

'It's the kind of thing you don't forget.'

'But you kept on visiting her. How many times a year?'

'I never counted.'

'Well, once a month?'

'Once. Or maybe twice.'

'Always at the same time of day?'

'Almost always. I finish work at six. And in summer, that would be about the time she came home.'

'Would she ask you to sit down?'

'I didn't wait to be asked. She was my aunt, after all.'

'And she was going to leave everything to you?'

'Yes.'

'Did you think about that?'

'I used to think it would make my life easier when I'm old. The profession of masseuse is a more tiring one than you might imagine. You need a certain amount of physical strength. In a few years, I'll be too old to carry on.'

'But in the meantime, did you ask her for money?'

'From time to time. Because in this job, there are sometimes dead seasons. During the summer holidays, for instance, when practically all my clients leave Paris, some of them for two or three months.'

'Did you ever quarrel with your aunt?'

'No, never.'

'And you never accused her of being mean?'

'No.'

'Did she know how you felt about her?'

'I suppose so.'

'And you knew she never kept much money at home?'

'Yes, I knew that.'

'Who took an impression of the front-door lock?'

'Not me.'

'Your lover, then.'

'He never said so to me.'

'But he did show you the key he had had cut?'

'No, I never had any key.'

'Look, here you are, telling lies again. Not only did you have a key to the apartment, you also had the one for your uncle Antoine's workshop across the corridor.'

She said nothing, like a stubborn child being scolded.

'I've got some bad news to pass on, and that might perhaps change your statement. I was in Toulon the day before yesterday.'

She gave a start. Though, as he knew, she was well aware where Marcel had gone.

'First of all, admit it: you two hadn't quarrelled at all, you hadn't really thrown him out.'

'Think what you like, I can't stop you.'

'This quarrel, supposedly because he was lazing about in bed, was staged for my benefit.'

She didn't move a muscle.

'I met him in Toulon. And of course, you know what he went to do there.'

'No.'

'Still lying? Down there, a few kilometres out of town, is a villa where a certain Pepito Giovanni lives. An ex-gangster, who has more or less bought his way out of trouble and is now into big business. I imagine Marcel must have worked for him at some point in the past, but he was a very small cog in that machine. Marcel was never a big-time gangster. Just a henchman, who had a few walk-on parts.'

A flash of anger crossed her features, but she made no protest.

'Do you agree with me?'

'I've nothing to say.'

'Please excuse me for a moment.'

He picked up the telephone and this time he got through to the examining magistrate.

'Maigret here. Can I come up and see you for a minute?'

'I'll be waiting. Better come straight away, because I have a witness to question in ten minutes.'

He left his interviewee alone with Lapointe, and went through the door to the Palais de Justice.

'How's the investigation going?'

'I hope I'm not getting ahead of myself, but I'm expecting to clear it up today. I went to Toulon on Saturday and a number of things happened there. I'll tell you about them later. But for the moment, I need an arrest warrant in the name of Angèle Louette.'

'Isn't that the niece?'

'Yes.'

'And you think she was the one who killed the old lady?'

'I don't know that yet, but I hope I soon will, one way or the other. That's why I'm not sure whether I'll use the warrant or not.'

'Hear that, Gérard? Can you make out the form?'

When Maigret returned to his office, it was as if the two people sitting there were waxworks.

He held out the warrant to Angèle.

'I presume you know what this is, and that you will understand why I asked you to bring a case with a change of clothes and whatever else you need.'

She did not reply or flinch.

'Now, to start with, we're going to talk about Marcel. I met him in a bar in Toulon, the Amiral, it's called, a place he knew well when he lived on the Côte d'Azur. He also knew very well a barman called Bob. Ever heard him mention the name?'

'No,' she spat out.

But her attention was aroused: she was waiting with visible anxiety to hear more.

'A bit player like Marcel wasn't going to be able to get a meeting immediately with a big fish like Giovanni. He needed a go-between, and Bob was the one. What he told Giovanni, I don't know. Marcel had something to sell, something very important, because this big crime boss agreed to see him the next day. Do you follow me?'

'Yes.'

'You've understood I'm talking about the revolver.'

'I've never seen this revolver you keep talking about. I've told you that more than once.'

'And every time, you've been lying. Well, Giovanni was so intrigued that he held on to the gun. I went to see him shortly afterwards, and we had a very interesting conversation. Among other things, I told him about the origin of the revolver, and the part that Marcel had played in the death of your aunt.

'You see, when a gangster has made his money and

more or less pulled out of criminal affairs, he doesn't like any hint of trouble.

'And Giovanni realized that being in possession of this gun would place him in serious jeopardy. I was no sooner out of the house than he jumped into his yacht and had his man sail him out to sea, so your uncle's famous revolver is now lying dozens of metres down below.'

Maigret emptied his pipe and filled another.

'Well, some other things happened in Toulon after I'd left. I only heard about them yesterday morning, when my colleague phoned me, soon after I saw you. But first, tell me again that there was no longer anything between you and Marcel, and that you had definitely shown him the door.'

'I'm waiting to hear what happened.'

'Well, Marcel himself was somewhat compromising. As they say in gangland, dead men tell no tales.'

'He's dead?'

She had stiffened suddenly and her voice had changed.

'But that doesn't affect you any more, does it?'

'What happened exactly?'

'Some time that night he was shot in the head, with a .38, the kind of gun used by professionals. He was found next morning floating in the harbour.'

'Is this a trap for me?'

'No.'

'You swear that on the head of your wife?'

'Yes, I swear.'

Then tears began rolling down her cheeks and she opened her handbag to take out a handkerchief.

8.

He went to stand at the window, to give her time to regain her self-possession. A light rain was still falling and umbrellas were glistening on the street below.

He heard her blow her nose, and when he returned to his seat, she was patting a little rouge on her cheeks.

'As you see, the whole affair fell through, and your aunt was killed for nothing.'

She was still sniffing and her hand trembled as she took out a cigarette and lit it.

'What remains to be ascertained is whether it was you or Marcel who smothered the old lady.'

Contrary to what he expected, she didn't reply at once. Wouldn't it have been easy for her to defend herself, now that her lover was out of the picture?

'As far as he is concerned, of course, there will be no further judicial inquiries. But it's not the same for you.'

'Why do you hate me so much?'

'I don't hate you. I'm trying to do my job as humanely as possible. From the very first day, you've been lying to me. So how do you expect me to take any other attitude towards you in the circumstances?'

'You knew I loved him.'

'And indeed I know that you still love him, even now he's dead.'

'Yes, that's true.'

'Why did you pretend to break up?'

'It was his idea. He was hoping to throw you off the track.'

'You knew what he was going to do in Toulon?'

She looked straight at him and, for the first time, she did not try to lie or dodge his question.

'Yes.'

'How long had you known about the revolver's existence?'

'About thirteen or fourteen years. I got on well with Uncle Antoine. He was a good sort, rather lonely. I don't think he had found my aunt the kind of companion he was hoping for. So he spent a lot of time shut up in his cubby hole.'

'Where you would go to see him?'

'Yes, quite often. That was his passion, and every year or so, he'd send one of his inventions to the Lépine competition.'

'So that's how you knew about the revolver?'

'I saw him work on it for about two years. He told me confidentially that there was a problem he had yet to resolve. "And if I do, one day, it'll make a lot of noise," he would say. Then he would laugh. "When I say make a noise, I mean the opposite. Do you know what a silencer is?"

' "Yes," I said. "I've seen them in films or on TV: a little thing you fix on the end of a gun so that people won't hear the shot."

' "Yes, that's it, more or less. Of course, you can't just walk into a shop and buy them, it's illegal. But suppose you didn't have to use a separate silencer, that it was part of the gun itself, concealed inside?"

'He was very excited.

' "I've almost managed it. Just a few more details to perfect. And when I sell the patent, all the guns they use in the police and the army will be silent." '

She remained without speaking for a while, then murmured:

'He died a few days later. I don't know anything about guns. And I forgot all about the famous revolver.'

'When did you tell Marcel about it?'

'A month ago, perhaps. Or no, three weeks. We were crossing the Pont-Neuf and I pointed to the windows on Quai de la Mégisserie. I said that's where my aunt lived, and that I'd inherit from her one day.'

'Why did you tell him about the inheritance?'

She blushed and looked away.

'To try and hang on to him.'

She had had no illusions.

'And a bit later, when we were sitting on a café terrace, I told him the story of the revolver, which I'd suddenly remembered. To my great surprise, he got very interested.

'He asked me if I'd seen the gun since my uncle's death.

' "No, I've never even been back into his workshop."

' "Did your aunt know about it?"

' "He might have mentioned it to her, but I dare say she paid it no more attention than I did. I'll ask her."

' "No, my dear Angèle," he said. "Don't do that. Don't mention it to her at all."

'I'm reporting our conversation as it happened, and it

163

may surprise you, but we were rather formal with each other. Except on rare occasions,' she said, with some embarrassment.

'Do you have a key to the apartment?'

'No.'

'Does the same key open the little cubby hole, as you call it?'

'No, there was a special key, but my aunt had it. Probably in her handbag. He didn't mention it for a few days. When I got home one night, he had two keys in his hand.

' "What do you want to do?"

' "Find that revolver."

' "What for?"

' "Because it's worth a fortune. When you know your aunt is out and won't come back, go and look in the apartment and the workshop."

' "But why would I? I'll inherit everything when she dies."

' "Oh, old grannies like her, they live for ever. You might have to wait another ten years, massaging all those middle-aged women." '

She looked at Maigret and sighed.

'Do you understand now? I didn't say yes right away. But I didn't want to lose him and he kept going on about it. In the end, I took the keys one afternoon. I saw my aunt go off towards the Tuileries, and I knew she wouldn't be back before six.'

'I began with the apartment. I looked everywhere, putting things back in their place.'

'Not carefully enough, obviously, because she noticed.'

'Then two days later, I looked in the cubby hole. In all, I went four times to Quai de la Mégisserie.'

'And Marcel?'

'Just once.'

'When?'

She turned her head away.

'The afternoon my aunt was killed.'

'What did he say to you when he got back?'

'I wasn't home. I'd been with a client since five thirty – the appointment had been postponed. It was a lady I've been going to for twenty years, Madame de la Roche, 61, Boulevard Saint-Germain.'

'And when did you get home?'

'At seven. She'd kept me talking as usual.'

'Why didn't you say before that you had an alibi?'

'Because that would have meant incriminating Marcel.'

'You preferred to be a suspect?'

'Well, as long as you were hesitating between the two of us . . .'

'So the gun *was* on top of your wardrobe?'

'Yes.'

'Your lover had found it in the bedside table?'

'Yes. It's the last place I'd have looked, because my aunt was scared stiff of firearms.'

'Lapointe, did you get that? You can go and type out the statement. But first, telephone Madame de la Roche, Boulevard Saint-Germain.'

They remained alone together, and he felt the need to stand up and go to the window again.

'As far as Marcel is concerned, the charges are completely

dropped,' he muttered, 'because we can't put a dead man on trial. But you're alive and well. You weren't a party to the old woman's death, that's true. Well, we'll soon find out about that.'

It was no longer the same woman that he now had in front of him. She had lost her stiff pose. Her features, like her strong body, seemed to have slumped.

There was a good five minutes' silence before Lapointe appeared again in the office.

'The lady confirms it,' he said simply.

'Thank you. Now do you see the situation you are in?'

'You made me read the arrest warrant, and I know what that means.'

'When I had it made out, I didn't yet know which of the two of you had killed your aunt.'

'Well, you know now.'

'You were not at the scene. The crime was not premeditated. So you couldn't have known it would take place. In other words, you are not a direct accomplice. What you could be accused of is not reporting your lover to the police, and keeping in your apartment stolen goods, namely a firearm.'

She maintained her neutral expression. It was as if life no longer interested her. She was far away, in Toulon perhaps, with Marcel.

Maigret went over to open the door into the inspectors' office. He spoke to the nearest one, who happened to be the burly Torrence.

'Can you come into my office for a moment? Don't you or anyone else leave until I get back.'

'Understood, chief.'

He went back up to the examining magistrate, who asked the witness he was questioning to step outside.

'Was it her, then?'

'No, she's got a cast-iron alibi.'

Maigret told him the whole story as quickly as possible. It still took a certain amount of time.

'There's no question of trying to charge Giovanni,' he murmured finally.

'No, we wouldn't get anywhere.'

'So all in all, she's no more guilty than he is.'

'You mean . . .?'

The magistrate scratched his head.

'Is that what you have in mind? You'd simply let her go?'

Maigret did not admit that this idea had come to him indirectly via Madame Maigret.

'We'd have to establish complicity, which wouldn't be easy, especially as the revolver has now completely disappeared.'

Another quarter of an hour passed before Maigret could go back down to the Police Judiciaire, since the magistrate insisted on consulting the public prosecutor.

It shocked Maigret a little to see Torrence sitting at his own desk, in his own chair.

'She hasn't budged, chief.'

'Has she said anything?'

'No, didn't open her mouth. Shall I go now?'

Angèle was looking at Maigret without curiosity, as if resigned to her fate.

'How old are you exactly?'

'Fifty-six. I don't usually own up to that, because some of my clients would find me too old.'

'Which apartment will you live in now, your own or your aunt's?'

She looked at him in astonishment.

'I don't have any choice, do I?'

He picked up the arrest warrant and tore it in half.

'You're free to go,' he said simply.

She didn't get up at once. It was as if her legs had suddenly turned to jelly. Tears rolled down her cheeks and she did not try to wipe them.

'I . . . I can't find the words . . .'

'Words won't be much use now. Come back this afternoon to sign the record of your statement.'

She stood up hesitantly and started towards the door.

'Your suitcase!' he reminded her.

'Oh, yes, I forgot . . .'

But there were so many things she would not forget!

OTHER TITLES IN THE SERIES

MAIGRET'S CHILDHOOD FRIEND
GEORGES SIMENON

'Florentin pulled one of those faces which had once amused his classmates so much and disarmed the teachers . . .

Maigret didn't dare to ask why he had come to see him. He studied him, struggling to believe that so many years had passed . . .

He was so used to acting the fool that his face automatically assumed comical expressions. But his face was still greyish, his eyes anxious.'

A visit from a long-lost schoolmate who has fallen on hard times forces Maigret to unpick a seedy tangle of love affairs in Montmartre, and to confront the tragedy of a wasted life.

Translated by Shaun Whiteside

OTHER TITLES IN THE SERIES

MAIGRET AND THE KILLER
GEORGES SIMENON

'*Leaning on the banisters, Madame Maigret watched her husband going heavily downstairs . . . what the newspapers didn't know was how much energy he put into trying to understand, how much he concentrated during certain investigations. It was as if he identified with the people he was hunting and suffered the same torments as they did.*'

A young man is found dead, clutching his tape recorder, just streets away from Maigret's home, leading the inspector on a disturbing trail into the mind of a killer.

Translated by Shaun Whiteside

INSPECTOR MAIGRET

OTHER TITLES IN THE SERIES

MAIGRET AND THE WINE MERCHANT
GEORGES SIMENON

'Maigret had never been comfortable in certain circles, among the wealthy bourgeoisie, where he felt clumsy and awkward . . . Built like a labourer, Oscar Chabut had hauled himself up into this little world through sheer hard work and, to convince himself that he was accepted, he felt the need to sleep with most of the women.'

When a wealthy wine merchant is shot in a Paris street, Maigret must investigate a long list of the ruthless businessman's enemies before he can get to the sad truth of the affair.

OTHER TITLES IN THE SERIES